Tales of
Cardinal Court

Tales of Cardinal Court

Gertrude Crocker

Tales of Cardinal Court

Paperback edition, 2020
ISBN: 978-1-941066-45-4

Library of Congress Control Number: 2020946541

Book design by Jo-Anne Rosen

Cover photo by Kevin Crocker

Wordrunner Press
Petaluma, California

To
Dale Schnell, Donna Lowe,
Inger Gleason and Patty Poindexter,
for all their valuable input and support.

Contents

Foreword

In sleepy Marin County, a new development on the outskirts of town is born and a plush golf course comes to life. Brown mega-mansions pop up randomly around its green edge and two "experimental homes" appear in the hills above.

An equally experimental string of 1440 square feet, two-story townhouses form a lazy semicircle around the 11th hole. They are condominium units – a first anywhere outside of Hawaii – and soon are filled with a restless mix of middle-class suburban pioneers.

JFK is alive and the Cold War is raging. The Seattle Space Needle shines brightly. Three inmates escape from Alcatraz and "Campbell Soup Cans" make Andy Warhol famous.

The future is bearing down on the residents of Cardinal Court, and only some of them know it.

It's 1962 – anything can happen.

Kevin Crocker – 2020

Tales of Cardinal Court

Moving In

Cardinal Court, a community of townhouses built around a curving bluff, looks over and beyond a golf course to a view of San Francisco Bay. In no way does it fit the definition of a court, but the wide dead end street is tree-shaded and lined with the greenest of lawns, all pleasing to behold. As Marianne Fallon, self-appointed social arbiter and custodian of its ultimate destiny reminds residents, "Cardinal Court is a most desirable place to live. Let's keep it that way."

And if golfing or tennis or swimming, or nothing more strenuous than soaking your bones in a spa is your fancy, Cardinal Court offers all of the above. Saturday morning lawn mowing is popular, too. And garage sales.

On an Autumn day a scratched and fender-dented moving van pulled up at Number 23 and Marianne Fallon hastened to snap the leash on Cookie's collar. She would walk her Doberman, and just by chance, just happening to be passing by, size up the movable chattels about to be unloaded. People's belongings said a lot about them, as did the battered van. The burly, tow headed driver and his muscular assistant probably didn't even notice the caked-on mud or the dents. Marianne tut-tutted her disapproval.

Cookie Fallon lifted a leg to leave a token of his visit on a tree shading Number 23's lawn. Marianne allowed him plenty of sniffing time, but when he signaled a desire to move on to the next tree on the next property she held the leash taut. "No, Cookie, Mommie's not going yet."

Her first impression of the newcomer was not good. Tacky! she pronounced the furniture, taking note of a plastic coffee table, three canvas-webbed aluminum-framed deck chairs, a slippery looking sofa, a pink shaded floor lamp. Tacky, tacky! Her disdain included a beat-up tomcat, slinking low from the open garage, ears back, to challenge Cookie. "Scat!" she hissed through her teeth, "Don't you dare come near my dog, you mangy beast!"

The tomcat ambled on with no loss of dignity, as if it had never entered his mind to mix it up with a dumb dog anyway.

Marianne lingered in the vicinity of Number 23 for as long as she could reasonably expect to pass for a person merely walking a dog. Anyone peering from the picture window might think she was nosy. She had better retreat now, drag the reluctant Cookie home.

Five minutes later she was on the horn, the broadcasting network of Cardinal Court, reporting to Joannie Dettner.

"Can you *believe* the stuff that's going in at Number 23? You can see it from your house, can't you? My God! It's strictly Early Salvation Army!"

"I know! It's incredible, isn't it? I'd say it's more like Period Dentist's Office. That couch made my teeth ache! And I saw *her* getting out of her car. She was kind of weaving."

"Really? Did you see a man around? I didn't. Another single female, do you think?"

"Yeah, it looks that way to me. Single and skinny and bleached, and maybe not too sober. Listen, hon, I'll call you back. I've got to call Lottie Dixon. She can see right into the kitchen."

"Okay, but you won't get much out of her. She saw everything when George and Linda lived there. Never said a word about it, remember?"

"Sure, I remember." Joannie giggled. "I guess she knew about their divorce before they did. Maybe I'll just drop in over there. See for myself." Phones were ringing and busy signals buzzing all over Cardinal Court. Gen McMurdo was telling Maggie Watson. "I just *happened* to be walking Mimi, you know? *She's* got this weird accent. She was talking to a scrawny cat meowing like mad and trying to claw its way out of a carrier. That's when I heard the accent."

"Oh, brother!" Maggie laughed. "Cookie Fallon's mommie is not going to like having a cat around. It might scratch her darling pet!"

By telephone, the good ladies of the court tried and convicted the new occupant of number 23 on clear evidence: Single, skinny and blonde, tacky furniture, weird accent, scrawny cat, questionable sobriety. No need to articulate the sentence tacitly agreed on: No one would ring her doorbell to bid her welcome; she would not be invited to join the Thursday morning coffee klatch.

In her new home, the latest stopping-off place since leaving Mallorca, Mona Lisa Svensen regarded the Rent-a-Suite furniture with disgust. How ugly it all was. How depressing. And if she had forgotten the vodka, left it at last night's motel, she just might cut her wrists.

She rummaged through a Gucci carryall dangling a "Miscellaneous" tag ... It's not here! ... Yes! Oh yes! ... I remember now ... I took a sip ... waiting for a red light to change ...

The bottle secured, Mona Lisa found a glass, a motel souvenir, in the carryall. She filled it for sipping and stood at the kitchen window staring out at the neglected back yard. Dead plants, foot-high weeds, tangled vines, overgrown shrubs. She thought of her beautiful terraced garden in Mallorca. Bougainvillea, olive trees, shy begonias hiding in shady places.

Six months ago she had called Mallorca home. How long did she live there, twenty years? And now this, this house bought sight unseen in a godforsaken suburb in a country no longer familiar to her. A home-away-from-home deemed to be suitable for the widow of a suicide.

She thought of Eric, her long-faced, suddenly oh-so-dutiful thirty-plus son, convincing her by transatlantic pleading to come back to the States. Perhaps he saw those long and costly telephone conversations as an investment. It wouldn't surprise her, either, if he had endowed himself a hefty broker's fee, lost in the stack of papers she signed to buy the house. That's what his father would have done.

Mona Lisa had to admit she didn't feel too motherly toward this young man, etched in her memory as a shivering little boy climbing out of a pool after a Red Cross swimming lesson, his eyes red with chlorine. Too much had separated them since that time: boarding schools since he was ten, and only occasional visits to Mallorca at Christmas or during summer vacations.

It's awful, she thought, but I just don't trust my own son. He has shifty eyes like Sven, his father. In his Welcome-home-Mother speech at the airport, Eric volunteered too readily to handle her financial affairs. He was willing and anxious to save her the bother, he said. Thank God her father had tied up her inheritance in a solid trust fund! Sven had tried to get at it, and failed. So naturally he had to blow his brains out.

Eric's concern for her welfare was too transparent to warm Mona Lisa's heart. He can't even get up a smile for his long lost mother, she thought. "Now that Dad's gone, Mother," (he carefully avoided reference to the way he went), "I'm going to take care of you. I want you to meet my good friend at the bank. You'll like him. And the house I found for you isn't far from mine. I want us to be a family, you and me and Betty." Betty, his wife, hadn't found it convenient to meet Mona Lisa as yet, and their home was in another town miles away. But certainly closer than Europe.

Mona Lisa roamed the half empty rooms of her new home. The odd pieces of rented furniture looked dejected, as though aware that nobody cared about or wanted them. Such trash, she muttered, I'm almost sorry for the poor things.

Soon, or sometime soon, or whenever, she would unpack the two suitcases and the bulging carryall she seemed to have been dragging around with her forever. Or six months anyway. All over Europe and finally to this friendless place, Cardinal Court, USA.

Back to the kitchen to refill her glass, she closed the blinds to shut out the ugliness of dead vegetation. Oh God, she prayed, will I ever see my cherished worldly goods again? Sleep in my own lovely bed? Packed and shipped and at sea long enough to have sailed twice around the Horn and back? Maybe the ship was sunk. Maybe all those treasures she and Sven had collected in the good days — the brocaded sofa and chairs, the silver candlesticks, the Venetian glass, the English bone china, the carpets and pictures — were all growing barnacles on the ocean floor.

She wandered into the living room and sat on the glossy vinyl-coated couch, but right away she began to slide off.

Stretching out full length, though, was not too bad. Carefully setting her glass conveniently near to her on the floor, she closed her eyes.

Well, she thought, at least I'm not traveling all over the map homeless anymore. Tomorrow, I'll go to the pound and get a dog. Everyone around here has a dog. Or else the same dogs kept passing back and forth when the truck was unloading. I'll get a big dog, big and mean looking, to keep the rabbit-eyed Doberman from wee-weeing on my tree. *She* didn't think I saw her letting him do it.

Whitey's too old to chase dogs anymore, but what a terror that cat was once! Those cold green eyes ... that unwavering stare ... and black as sin. Dogs thought twice about mixing it up with Whitey.

Any chance of meeting someone interesting here, I wonder? I doubt it. I'll bet they're all dedicated husbands. Dedicated to commuting and mowing their lawns.

But the man who delivered this so-called furniture ... Gunlak something ... where did I put the card he gave me? I liked his looks. Nice smile. A Swede like me, maybe? Gunlak sounds like a Norwegian name, though. Suppose I call him up? Ask him to deliver my stuff if the ship ever gets here?

Battle-scarred Whitey, old as God and minus one green eye, jumped on Mona Lisa's stomach. Absently, she stroked his rough coat.

Big Dog Small Fire

The square-chested, bowlegged English bull dog was awaiting extinction in the incinerator at the Humane Society when Mona Lisa Svensen rescued it. The dog won her heart when he licked her fingers through the wire cage, wagging a stump of tail so furiously his whole hind end jiggled.

Looking straight into his eyes she communicated her thoughts: Listen, dog … somehow you remind me of Sven. My husband had eyes like yours, sort of anxious but hopeful. But that was only just before he … well … we don't want to think about that now, do we? I was really looking for a younger dog. You're a little long in the tooth, and I doubt if you'd be a match for that stupid Doberman down the street. But you like me and I like you. I think I'll call you Sven Two.

Sven Two was happy with his new home. The good ripe smell of the ratty old fur coat Mona Lisa got at Goodwill for his bed pleased him, and Whitey, her elderly black cat, decided to be philosophical about the presence of a rival too big to climb into his spot on Mona Lisa's lap. Whitey even condescended to sleep with him on the new bed with the lovely smell.

Mona Lisa tugged Sven Two's leash. "Not that tree, old dog, that's our tree. I've told you before, Number 23 is our house, and that's our tree. We'll go down the block. You can leave your calling card on somebody else's tree."

Sven Two looked worried, but that was natural. His deeply furrowed brow, set in a permanent frown, made him look that way. The glad wagging of his bit of tail expressed his true feelings. Any tree was okay with him, and there were plenty of trees down the block.

They hadn't gone far when he sat down, tilted his head and sniffed. Mona Lisa tugged impatiently but Sven Two was adamant. Something in the air had stopped him cold. Then Mona Lisa sniffed. She smelled smoke. Sven Two broke loose from her grip on the leash and tore home, instinctively seeking a safe place should the smoke he smelled mean fire.

At Number 16, across the street, smoke poured from an open upstairs window. A flaming curtain billowed out, igniting the wood frame which sent tongues of fire to the eaves.

Mona Lisa saw Marianne Fallon walking her Doberman, at a safe distance from Sven Two. She heard her cry FIRE! and saw her run. Thinking Marianne intended to turn in the alarm, Mona Lisa followed Sven Two to Number 23.

From her living room window she watched a drama unfold at Number 16. Sven Two watched with her. A barefoot young man scrambled out the door, holding up his pants with one hand, struggling to get his shirt on with the other. A window, not the one on fire, was flung open and a disembodied hand dropped two shoes into a rhododendron bush. Retrieving the shoes, the young man made a dash for a Shell Oil Co. pickup truck parked at the curb. He yanked the door open, jumped in, and drove off in great haste.

Then fire engines clanged into Cardinal Court and a young woman appeared at the door left open by the hasty young man.

She too was shoeless, slightly disheveled but otherwise almost fully dressed. She fumbled with the buttons on her blouse. Mona Lisa heard her shrill scream, "My house is on fire!"

"As if the fire laddies couldn't figure that one out for themselves," Mona Lisa remarked to Sven Two.

From the vantage point of her living room window she watched a representative group of the ladies of the Court assemble to witness the event. Had she been closer she would have heard these ladies intone their lines like a Greek chorus:

Joannie Dettner: "Debbie ought to be ashamed of herself. That kid pumps gas at the Shell station."

Marianne Fallon: "I know. I saw them falling all over each other there once when I stopped for gas."

Maggie Watson (reflectively): "He's kinda cute though."

Gen McMurdo: "I swear to God anyone wearing pants gets invited in. Don't tell *me* it's just for a cup of coffee."

Lottie Dixon: "Maybe she can't help herself. Maybe she's one of those nympho ... *you* know ... phobics? ... or whatever you call 'em."

Joannie Dettner (with a sad shake of her head): "Poor Harvey. Somebody ought to tell him."

Gen McMurdo: "Oh yeah? Harvey's got a short fuse. I wouldn't want Debbie's blood on *my* hands. And next time, Marianne, ring the door bell before you turn in the alarm. Give the kids a chance to get their shoes on."

The fire was quickly extinguished. An electric heater had been left burning near a bathroom towel rack under a curtain. As fires go, it wasn't much. More smoke than flames. Rather disappointing, in fact, for the assembled ladies of the Court.

Mona Lisa noticed that none of these ladies stepped forward to comfort the dejected young woman sitting on the doorstep with her head in her hands.

"Poor little Mrs. Number 16," she said to Sven Two. "She's being ignored. But I bet they'll all be watching behind their curtains when her husband comes home." She scratched the dog fondly under the chin. "I know what you're thinking, my friend. That I've been watching too? Right? Well, how about yourself? Isn't that why you've got your paws on the window sill?"

Sven Two yawned. Whitey strolled into the room and sat on Mona Lisa's foot. "Ah, so there you are, my dear cat! You missed it! Oh well. We'll never know the real story anyway. Like who was that boy who didn't have time to put his shoes on?"

Whitey arched his back and rubbed against her leg. "We're ostracized, you know," she went on, "you and me and Sven Two. And I think Mrs. Number 16 is now in the same boat. What do you say we ask her over for a drink? Maybe she'd like to talk to somebody about what happened."

Whitey dropped to the floor and rolled over. Mona Lisa stroked his belly with the toe of her shoe. "You favor that idea, do you? Well, maybe we will some day."

She walked into the kitchen. "Let's all have a drink," she said. "Just ourselves. Right now." Sven Two yawned again and Whitey ambled off. "No? Really? None for you two? Okay, I won't insist. To each his own, I always say."

Mona Lisa was wrong about Mrs. Number 16 being in her boat. For a while the ladies of the court were cool to Debbie, but stopped short of setting her adrift, for fear of offending Harvey, a "high level executive" in a "major corporation."

Debbie's husband wore confidence-inspiring three-piece suits and served Chivas Regal (he called it "Chivvy") at parties.

His grey Mercedes and Debbie's red Porche were tangible and impressive proof of his worth. Harvey was a prince, if not a captain, of industry. A definite asset to Cardinal Court.

The only character flaw the ladies could attribute to this capital fellow was his volatile temper. It was rumored that he had pushed Debbie around for far lesser crimes than burning up his bathroom.

Bonding in sisterhood they resolved to protect Debbie. Gen McMurdo phoned Maggie Watson who phoned Marianne Fallon who phoned ...and so on. "I hear Harvey is furious! He's ready to kill her! It's up to us to make sure he never gets wind of anything. We won't say *word one* about the gas pumper, see? Listen! What he doesn't know won't hurt him, okay?"

So Harvey was kept in ignorance. He never knew that the young man who pumps gas at the Shell station fled from his house, shoeless and half shirtless, just ahead of the fire engines.

Mona Lisa and Sven Two, who saw it all, never said *word one* either.

Going to the Dogs

Jessie Donley, matriarch of Cardinal Court, held a cigarette between her thumb and index finger. Her middle, ring and pinkie fingers curved in a graceful arc. Cautiously, as if on the off chance it might explode, she touched it to her lips, puffed and blew.

Kate Kardis, leaning back on Jessie's sofa with her feet on the coffee table, watched the amateur performance with amusement.

"You ought to quit that habit, Jess, it'll ruin your lungs."

Jessie adjusted her E-Z-BOY lounger a notch. "I like it. It's comforting. Your company isn't exactly scintillating today, you know. What's the problem, dearie? You're miles away and I'm lonely."

"Oh Lord, I'm sorry, Jessie! I didn't sleep much last night. I just couldn't get those damn ashes off my mind. Rattling and rolling in the back of the station wagon. It's driving me crazy. I feel like I've been hauling that stupid can around forever. What am I going to do about it, Jess? Tell me what I should do!"

"Really, Kate, it seems to me I've heard that song before. I've already told you. At least fifty times. You've simply got to scatter them someplace or bury them in the back yard."

"Oh yeah? So the dogs can dig them up? And just exactly where is this 'someplace' supposed to be located? Golden Gate

Park, maybe? The Pacific Ocean? With my luck, I'd probably get arrested for littering. Anyway, the whole idea gives me the creeps. It's too much like tossing out garbage or something."

Kate's champion hole-diggers, Blossom and Twinkie, a matched pair of basset hounds whose fat bellies skimmed the ground, were tied — quite tranquilly — to Jessie's sidewalk mail box whenever Kate came by for a visit. Jessie hated dogs.

"Listen, Kate," she said, "I know you're right about the dogs. Forget what I said about the back yard. But, I also know you're broke, or close to it. So I'm going to buy you an urn. Don't shake your head at me! I insist! You can keep it on your mantelpiece like an icon. It's just plain *indecent*, you know, to keep Duke, or anyone else, in a coffee can."

"I know that! It was supposed to be temporary. I was going to buy an urn myself, at first, but I changed my mind. Right now I wouldn't buy him an urn if I won the lottery! And don't you dare buy one either."

It was sundown at Cardinal Court and Jessie and Kate were fifteen minutes into their regular observance of Happy Hour. Kate got up to refill the glasses, pouring Ancient Age over ice, adding a dollop of water and stirring the finished product with her little finger.

She carried her drink to the sliding glass doors, looked down at the 11th hole of the golf course, watched a foursome putting on the green. She spoke with her back to Jessie: "I've got to tell you something, Jess." She took a deep breath that turned into a long sigh, and continued, "I know you'll think I'm heartless, but well ... I got this idea last night ... when I couldn't sleep ... thinking and thinking ... Oh, maybe I shouldn't tell you, Jess!"

"Maybe you should. Just tell me, Kate. Turn around and tell me. What's the point of talking to a window?"

"Okay, I will then. It's crazy, I guess, but last night it just came to me. This idea, I mean. Right out of the blue, like a bolt! ... What if I buried Duke in a dog and cat cemetery?"

Jessie grabbed the handle of her E-Z BOY lounger and propelled herself two notches forward for a closer look at Kate. She uttered a shocked "Omigod!" and fanned her face with a paper napkin.

"Would you run that by me again, dearie? Something about a *dog* and *cat* cemetery? That's what you said, isn't it?" Then she began to laugh, and unable to control the laughter, it continued until her whole body was shaking helplessly. "What an idea!" she managed to gasp. "An inspiration!" She wiped tears from her eyes with the paper napkin, took a reviving sip of her drink, blew her nose in a fresh paper napkin. "But you're not serious, of course."

"Oh but I am! Or I guess I am. Or kind of, anyway. Duke was a liar and a cheat. What right would a man like that have to complain about where he's buried?"

"All too true, dearie," Jessie said. "The best thing that man ever did was keel over with a heart attack, and all you got out of it was custody of his dogs and a two pound can of ashes. I think I'm beginning to cotton to the idea. There's a kind of poetic justice about a dog lover being buried in a dog cemetery."

"Yeah. That's what I said to myself last night. Wasn't he crazy about dogs? Didn't he dote on Blossom and Twinkie? Didn't he stuff them with goodies until they could barely waddle down the street?"

"So the idea gets better and better. It would be a decent enough burial. Just bye-bye Duke and may the Lord have mercy on your soul, you dog, you. And anyway, everybody thinks he was buried a year ago."

Kate said, "Then you don't really think it's too awful a thing to do, Jess?"

Jessie notched back, relaxed and smiling. "Just hand me the phone book, Katie. It's in the top drawer of the desk."

The yellow pages listed a handful of pet cemeteries. They chose "Peaceful Pets" in the East Bay as an ideal locale. No one they knew ever went to the East Bay. They would be incognito.

Jessie said that the thing to do was not think about it too much. Just do it. Before they could think of fifty reasons not to do it. "We'll go tomorrow," she said. Kate agreed. "Okay, I'm willing if you are. The sooner the better."

She freshened the drinks and sat back on the sofa, her feet in their usual place on the coffee table. The friends began to rehash, as a suitable topic for the occasion (which in a way could pass for a wake), the story of how Duke romanced Kate on the heels of his first wife's funeral. What they said about him was the only eulogy Duke was likely to get.

Duke had always had a "case" on Kate, dating back to when they were young and often turned up at the same parties, though never together. They both married, and both were eventually widowed.

Duke's first wife left her substantial estate to her grown children, his stepchildren, so he needed a new home. He recalled his old passion for Kate. Her husband was dead.

Duke made his move. He dazzled her with a whirlwind courtship climaxed by a whirlwind European honeymoon. For nine days the newlyweds viewed the Old World through the road-grimed window of a tour bus. Most of the time Kate had not an inkling of what country they happened to be passing through, since Duke kept plying her with copious amounts of champagne. On their return home, Duke even bought a Cardinal Court house. "A wedding present," he said, "all paid for, no mortgage."

There was hell to pay when it later developed that the trip to Europe and the champagne had been financed by siphoning off funds from the stepchildren's inheritance. The two irate stepchildren accused innocent Kate of conspiring with the real culprit, who had managed to avoid this unpleasant situation by dropping dead over Kate's kidney-shaped coffee table.

Duke's sins were uppermost in the friends' minds when they approached the gates of "Peaceful Pets" the next day. They were feeling almost sanguine about his coming disposal. Kate was in charge of the coffee can and Jessie carried a paper bag containing certain artifacts: a box of Doggie Treats, a chewed-on plastic bone, a tooth-marked red rubber ball and a worn leash, items the property of Blossom and Twinkie which were to go into the ground with their late master as tokens of authenticity.

An attendant with an appropriately solemn mien greeted them, eying the coffee can with suspicion. "How may I help you ladies?" he asked.

Kate was suddenly overcome by last-minute qualms. She answered in a small shaky voice, "We would like to bury this … eh … can … I mean inter these … whatdoyoucallem? … remains?"

The attendant's sober face registered his distaste for coffee cans as sepulchers for dead pets. "I see," he said. "But since your animal is already cremated, perhaps you would prefer an interment? We have some very nice urns."

Jessie, worried about Kate's attack of nerves, intervened. "My friend doesn't like urns. She wants him buried. In the ground."

16

"Very well, then. Just as you say. Please excuse me for a moment." The attendant entered a door marked "Office" and returned with a clipboard. A fresh form was on it, and he held a ballpoint pen at the ready. "Now, may I have your pet's name? A dog, I take it?"

Kate, encouraged by Jessie's calm directness, answered, "His name was Duke. And yes, he was a dog."

The attendant wrote "Duke" on the form and check marked "Dog." "Do you wish to have dates on the tombstone? In Loving Memory Of? Anything like that?"

In case Kate didn't see the pitfall ahead, Jessie blurted out, "Hey! Hold it right there, Buster! Who said anything about a tombstone?"

"Buster's" eyebrows raised a full inch. "Well, madam," he said stiffly, "It's the usual alternative to an urn, isn't it?"

The friends' eyes met in silent communication. This "usual alternative" sounded expensive. But to Jessie's surprise, Kate came up with an answer. ("Right out of the blue like a bolt," as she said later.) She beamed at the attendant as if understanding his problem and forgiving him for having it. "Oh, of course! I'm quite aware of that. But you see, it's against our religion. It doesn't go in for frivolities. Like tombstones and things? It's very strict about stuff like that."

"Frivolities?" The attendant's eyes swept over an ocean of small monuments silhouetted against tall trees and neatly aligned on a deep-green lawn. "Frivolities indeed!"

Jessie took over the deteriorating interview. "How about something ... well ... say in plastic? Suppose you just write 'Duke' on it? No Loving Memory or anything like that."

The attendant tore off the form, crumpled it up and threw it on the ground. "We don't have much call for plastic here,

17

but we may have a flat plaque lying around somewhere. I'll take a look. Excuse me."

"Don't bother," Jessie said. "We'll take it. Right now we're in kind of a hurry." She turned to Kate, smiling sweetly. "Give the man the can, dearie." Kate handed over Duke's dust, under dust to lie. Holding it gingerly, the attendant weighed the can in his hands. "My, it's heavy, isn't it? Must have been a very big ....."

Jessie interrupted, "Oh, didn't we mention that? Duke was a Great Dane."

"Ah. I see. Well then, if you'll step into my office I'll figure the cost of this ... eh ... simple interment."

The bill was presented and Kate wrote a check. She mentioned that the cost seemed excessive for the modest disposal of Duke's ashes, but the attendant refused to knock off a cent.

On the trip back to Cardinal Court the station wagon was blessedly free of the rattle of a rolling can. Kate wondered aloud if her check would bounce. "Last time I looked, the balance was pretty low."

"So what if it does," Jessie comforted her. "He's probably thrown the can in the trash by now anyway."

Kate laughed. "Poor Duke. Serves him right, I guess. Oh Lord! I just about died when you called that guy 'Buster'"

Jessie laughed with her. "Yeah. I surprised myself when I said it. But wasn't he a pompous ass?" She raised a hand to wave dismissal of all the world's pompous asses, and exclaimed, "Look, Kate! Look at my hand! I've still got the bag! Good God, I forgot to give it to him! I'm still holding the artifacts!"

Wedding Bells

Some time after Mona Lisa Svensen's move to Cardinal Court and the fire at number 16, Marianne Fallon and Joannie Dettner penetrated Jessie Donley's private sanctum by means of leaning stubbornly on her doorbell.

"Keep ringing, Joannie," Marianne insisted, "we know she's there and Kate Kardis is with her. Maybe the TV's on and they don't hear the bell. Push harder."

"Oh, sure!" Joannie jabbed the bell again. "Either they can't hear or they just don't want to open the door."

But Marianne, determined not to be ignored or rebuffed, said, "Try knocking. The bell could be out of order."

Jessie Donley's fame had preceded her to Number 24 Cardinal Court. She had been something of a celebrity during her husband's time in Washington, DC, his official hostess at important political receptions and social gatherings.

After Ed Donley's death she left Washington, and had barely finished unpacking her belongings at Number 24 when late one afternoon Marianne Fallon led a coterie of the neighborhood elite to call on her. Marianne was avid for the lowdown on Everybody Who Was Anybody in the Nation's Capital, and Jessie was an unimpeachable source. And besides,

Marianne hoped to "cultivate" Jessie if only to hobnob with a genuine celebrity.

Jessie answered their questions courteously that day but revealed nothing. When the visitations continued she grew tired of hedging and circumventing and her front door stayed shut, to be opened only to Kate Kardis's ring: one-long-and-two-short. Of all the ladies of Cardinal Court only Kate suited Jessie and only Jessie suited Kate.

Stretched out on her E-Z Boy lounger, Jessie banged down her highball glass with a thump. "That ringing and pounding is getting on my nerves! Kate, did you ever hear of those mirrors ... I think they were called 'busybodies'? You could see who was at your front door and across the street and down the block? I wonder ... do you think they still exist?"

"You don't need mirrors, Jess. All you have to do is peek between the drapes like I do. And anyway, we don't need to *see* them, do we? We already know who's making the racket."

"Those damn dogs of your are a dead giveaway, Kate. Our pesty friends are not going to go away. Next thing we know they'll be calling the police." Jessie struggled out of the lounger and headed for the door, muttering dramatically, "Lordy, Lordy! Oh Lord why doest thou persecutest me?"

Kate laughed and added, "*Ora pro nobis, Lord.*" She gathered up the glasses and the bottle of Old Crow and stowed the evidence under the kitchen sink. By the time Jessie had admitted the unwelcome callers Kate was back on the sofa with her feet on the coffee table, idly flipping the pages of a magazine.

Jessie greeted Marianne and Joannie with restrained cordiality: Oh yes, the bell *did* sometimes fail to ring, and sad to say, she and Kate were both a little hard of hearing. Yes indeed.

The ladies sat, crossed their legs and leaned back, ready for a chat about old times in DC. But first the local news, the fire at Number 16. Jessie was warned (Kate was ignored as a nonperson) not to breathe a word of what really caused the fire in Harvey and Debbie's bathroom. Harvey would simply murder Debbie if he found out. They went on to list Debbie's shortcomings in the morals department.

Jessie covered a yawn and murmured politely, "Excuse me." Kate grinned behind the pages of her magazine.

Jessie hadn't reacted to the scandal at Number 16 as expected, so Marianne switched to criticism of the newcomer on the block, Mona Lisa Svensen, she of the tacky furniture and the funny accent.

Joannie said, her eyes bright with indignation, "She just doesn't fit in here. I don't suppose you saw the *junk* that went into that house? Marianne thinks she's some kinda refugee or something. I say, sure she is. She's a refugee from outer space." She laughed alone at her witticism. Even Marianne scowled, sensing that Jessie was not amused. It was frustrating. Jessie seemed bored and it looked like they'd never get to the down and dirty stuff in Washington, because Jessie appeared to be falling asleep in her lounger.

But Jessie was still alert enough to look at her wrist-watch, put it to her ear and listen to it tick, as if checking to see if it had stopped. She yawned again, a frank whole-hearted gape this time not covered by a hand or followed by an excuse.

"You look tired, Jessie. Maybe we should *all* go and let you get some rest," Marianne said, glancing meaningfully at Kate, including her in the general exodus. But Kate, absorbed in her reading, didn't get the hint.

21

As Jessie was seeing them to the door, Kate got up, and on her way to the kitchen to retrieve the Old Crow, she called, "Bye-bye, girls. Be seein' ya!"

Jessie returned to the lounger, tilting it to Recline. She accepted the drink Kate offered, sighing, "What bores those women are! Why did I ever let them in? But this terrible Mona Lisa person ... I have a hunch I'd like her. Do you know who she is, Kate?"

"I run into her once in a while, walking the dogs. She's nice, Jess. She has this bulldog, but you wouldn't hold that against her, would you?" Kate smiled fondly at her friend. Jessie's fear and loathing of dogs was legendary.

"A bulldog! My god, aren't they vicious?"

"This one's too old to hurt a flea, Jessie. And Mona Lisa ... well, she's very pretty ... younger than us ... fortyish maybe ... and no accent. None at all. How would those snobs know how she talks anyway? They have never even spoken with her. She told me so herself."

"Really? That's pretty mean, isn't it. So why don't you and I do something about this situation. Call her, Kate. Ask her to come over."

The invitation delighted Mona Lisa. "You mean now? Right this minute? Oh, I'd love to! I've been sitting here looking at the wall, wondering what to do with myself. Number 24? I'll be right there."

After that first visit, three-person afternoon soirees became a regular event. Mona Lisa's irreverent attitude toward things the ladies of the court held dear amused Jessie and Kate, and she was awarded one-long-and- two-short bell ringing privileges, and very soon Mona Lisa's personal vodka bottle flanked the Old Crow under the kitchen sink at Number 24.

She told them how lonely she had been. "I thought of cutting my throat, but it's awfully messy. I like things neat. Besides, what would become of my dog, Sven Two, and poor old Whitey the Cat?"

A few months passed. Mona Lisa seemed to have something on her mind, something she wanted to say, but couldn't or wouldn't. Then one day she made an announcement. "I've been seeing somebody! Isn't it exciting? It's supposed to be a secret but I've got to tell you! How can I keep a secret from my dear friends? I'm engaged! To be married!"

"So that's it," Kate said. "We wondered what was eating you. So tell us, who's the lucky man?" And Jessie added, "Yes, tell us. Tell us everything, like where you met him and so forth. All the details. The who and the what and especially the why. Are you tired of single bliss?"

"I've been dying to tell you! The way it happened … I must be crazy …"

"Sounds like you're crazy about each other," Kate said.

"Oh, I am! He is! We are! But my son Eric is livid. He says I must be 'some kind of nut case.' His very words. But that's not what actually bothers him. You see, I haven't made a Will. He knows it and it worries him." She laughed. "That's my darling boy!"

"How come you told him this big secret in the first place?" Jessie asked.

"I didn't tell him. He walked in one day and there was Gunlak — that's his name, Gunlak Johansen — sitting there with his shoes off. Eric turned green! He recognized him as the man who delivered my furniture. Both times. First the rented stuff, then my own. Gunlak's shoes were off because his feet ache from hauling tons of furniture all day."

"Oh? So you're engaged to marry the moving man, are you?" Jessie looked at Kate, raising eloquent eyebrows. "I see. I must say it does seem rather an odd thing to do. I can imagine why Eric ... well ... what do you say Kate?"

"I say terrific! I say I'm happy for her! So tell! What's this Gunlak like?"

"He's nice. You'll like him. You've got to! Good looking, too. He's big, lots of muscles because of his line of work. Maybe a little younger than I, but who cares?" She beamed joyously at her friends. "And he's a Swede like me!"

"I like him already," Kate said. "So will Jessie when she gets to know him. I guarantee it."

Jessie asked, "Does this big, strong, handsome Swede fellow have a dog?"

Mona Lisa kept Kate and Jessie posted on the affair with the moving man, issuing almost daily bulletins right up to the actual setting of the date.

"And you two are going to be my bridesmaids. Say you will!"

Kate searched Jessie's face for a clue, but Jessie, laid back in the Recline position, her hands folded on her round stomach, merely smiled like a benign lady Buddha.

"You don't need two bridesmaids," Kate said. "Why don't you ask Jessie? She'd love it. She's very romantic, underneath it all."

Jessie beamed her kindly smile at Kate. "Oh no, dearie. I'm too old. But you'd be absolutely perfect for the job."

Son Eric's home in Tiburon was to be the wedding site, a gesture designed to remind his mother that he was her loving son and, so far, her only legitimate heir. Jessie would be the only guest besides the principals. She would drive herself to the ceremony in her ancient Buick because, as she said, one never knows when one might wish to make a quick getaway from certain events. Kate Kardis would deliver the bride-and-groom- to-be, and later Eric would take them to the honeymoon destination, the Fairmont Hotel.

Once Kate had been elected bridesmaid, whether or no, she threw herself into the role. At Macy's she found a flowery pink print dress and matching pumps with two inch heels. A pair of short white cotton gloves completed the outfit. Jessie remarked that Kate's new perm and red-gold tint plus all that pinkyness made her look like somebody's fairy godmother. "And of course," she said, "you know you'll never wear that dress again, or those ridiculous shoes either."

"Oh, I don't know, Jess," Kate replied airily, "I think my new look is quite chic. May I ask what you plan to wear? That old grey number, I suppose? That ties in a bow at the neck?"

"You suppose right, dearie. It's my best dress. What else would I wear?" She held out her empty glass. "Here, brides-maid, your turn."

"Isn't it always?" Grinning, Kate reached for the glass.

The wedding was scheduled for two o'clock. At twelve-thirty, Kate was pinkly dressed and off to help the bride get organized.

A beaming bridegroom, in a colorful kimono which may once have belonged to the late Sven One, flung open the door when Kate rang the bell at number 23. Kate and Gunlak hadn't actually met before, but he embraced her ardently.

"I'm Johansen! You're Kate! Come in! Toast the bride!" He led her to a chair and handed her a glass of vodka as he sang in a resonant baritone "...so for Gawd's Sake Get Me to the Church on Time!" as if taking up the tune where he left off to answer the doorbell.

Mona Lisa came into the room wearing a brief teddy and waving a glass. "Oh Kate! Don't you look beautiful! And isn't it a lovely day for a wedding? You've met him? My intended, shall we say?" She was all smiles and, as Kate noticed, a little giddy from vodka.

Kate put down her glass to take off her white gloves. "Oh lord, you haven't even begun to get dressed! For heaven's sake let's get going. We're supposed to be in Tiburon by two o'clock, remember?"

"I'm Getting Married in the Morning ..." sang Gunlak. He picked Mona Lisa up and whirled her around and around the room. "Put me down, you big lummox," she squealed and the two of them collapsed on a tapestry sofa that had finally made it Around the Horn. They kissed passionately with no perceptible inhibition and Kate stared at a painting on the wall to avoid the appearance of voyeurism. Still looking at the wall she said, "Listen you lovebirds, if you don't intend to get married today, I'm going home."

Gunlak jumped up, pulling Mona Lisa with him. "Don't go, Kate. Please? Don't worry. Plenty of time. Just give us a few minutes, okay?" He lifted up his giggling bride-to-be and carried her off, presumably to the bedroom.

Kate swallowed her drink and poured another from the bottle Gunlak had left conveniently near. "To calm my nerves," she muttered to herself. "My God! At a time like this ... to disappear ... we'll never make it to Tiburon on time ... am I the only one who takes this wedding seriously?"

Sharp little cries and sounds of vigorous activity emanated

from the presumed bedroom. Kate drank more vodka and waited, muttering to herself: "I wonder if Macy's would take this dumb dress back."

Kate didn't get the happy couple "to the church on time." It was three o'clock when they arrived at Eric's house, where Jessie, sitting stiffly in a chair since two o'clock, was praying for Kate to come and rescue her from the family dog. The big old collie had taken to her, looking soulfully into her face with rheumy eyes and shoving his muzzle on her lap. A recruited clergyman sat opposite, with little to say. Eric and his wife, Betty, side by side on the sofa, were tense, deep in gloom. What with no Will and the threat of a new and possibly sole heir, they were not feeling up to making small talk.

As Kate's car pulled up outside, a vibrant voice was heard. " ...in the Morning, Church Bell are Going to Ring ..." Eric opened the door.

Mona Lisa was wearing an embroidered silk sari, a souvenir of foreign travels. Gunlak's furniture-mover's muscles bulged in a tight blue suit that could have been a relic of his Confirmation. Kate's pink finery was beginning to droop.

The clergyman consulted his watch and ordered the ceremony to begin immediately. Except for a minor mishap, it went off well. Mona Lisa, a little unsteady on her feet, happened to totter forward and fall into the arms of the clergyman, who was obliged to hold her up for the space of two "I do's." And when Gunlak, sweating in his tight suit, lunged to her aid, all three came close to falling to the floor. But Eric, doubling as best man and giver-away of the bride, cried, "Steady on there now!" and order was restored.

The wedding cake sent the bride into raptures. "Happy

27

Wedding Cake to Me! I mean us! Gunlak and me!" she sang. "Everybody sing to our beautiful cake!" The little assembly made a stab at it, but though the tune was the familiar Happy Birthday, the words didn't seem to fit, and the singing petered out.

Jessie had offered to provide the bridal bouquet, and now suddenly remembered leaving it in her car. She sent Kate to retrieve the exotic orange lilies she had chosen, and when Mona Lisa breathed their perfume, orange pollen stuck to her nose. She tossed the bouquet to Kate, and orange pollen stuck to the pink dress. "You're next, dear Kate! The bridesmaid is always next!" Kate made a futile effort to brush off the sticky stuff. Macy's would never take back the dress now.

Champagne glasses were laid out on a buffet, and eying them, Gunlak called out, "Toast the bride! Let's all toast the bride!"

Eric signaled Betty for a private word. "Get them to cut the cake, will you? Let's get this charade over with, for Pete's sake."

"All right. You pour the wine. Not that your mother and your new stepfather need it."

Eric's mouth opened in shock. "My stepfather? My God, that never even occurred to me. He is, isn't he? Good Lord!"

"Indeed he is. But anyway, we can be glad your mother is paying for this shindig. She can afford it. She's loaded."

Eric spouted out a sour laugh. "Yeah, she's loaded all right. In more ways than one."

The refreshments were served, and Kate and Jessie left, carrying small boxes of wedding cake to dream on. Gunlak's "I'm getting Married in the Morning ..." still rang in their ears as they drove back to Cardinal Court in their separate cars.

The bridesmaid kicked off her pink pumps and elevated her feet to the coffee table. The wedding guest sank back on her E-Z Boy lounger, adjusted it to Recline and groaned, "Oh my God what a day." Their eyes met over their highball glasses and they broke into laughter.

"Poor Eric, he could hardly wait to get rid of us." Kate giggled, blotting tears on the sleeve of her pink dress. "And oh Jessie ... you don't know the half of it."

"Neither do you. For example, do you know I had to fend off that monster of a dog for a solid hour? And Gunlak ... he drove me crazy with that damn singing. Apparently he only knows one song. So what's your half I don't know?"

Kate's laughter was punctuated with hiccups. "You ... hic ... will never ... hic ... believe it."

"Try me. What happened before the main event that made you so late? Before they almost knocked over that poor preacher. And stop that hiccupping. Hold your breath and say The Our Father or something."

Kate managed to control her hiccups but not her giggles. "Well, to begin with, I rang Mona Lisa's bell ... all charged up for a wedding ... and Gunlak opened the door ... and then ..."

Listening, Jessie assumed her lady Buddha pose, sometimes smiling benignly, sometimes nodding solemnly, as Kate related the pre-nuptial details.

Poverty Road

To hear Edgar Longstreet tell it, Poverty Road was only a stone's throw from number 17 Cardinal Court, and the threat of ending up in the mythic place clouded Frances Longstreet's days and sometimes her nights. In a recurring dream, she and Edgar walked to the edge of a cliff where below them in a cluster of mean streets lay Poverty Road. They stood one false step away from their ultimate home.

Fran's chronic poorness embarrassed her. When certain ladies of the court made friendly overtures, inviting her to lunch with them or to come to the Thursday Morning Koffee Klatch, she declined, ashamed of not being able to reciprocate. The ladies thought they had been snubbed; their feelings were hurt and thereafter they treated her coldly.

"Just who does she think she is, anyway?" snapped Marianne Fallon. "Why, I happen to know *he's* barely making ends meet these days. I heard he hasn't got a pot to you-know-what in."

"Who told you that?" Joannie Dettner asked.

"Oh, he's always moaning and groaning about it on the golf course, telling people his hog belly business is about to bottom out. Did you ever *hear* of hog bellies before? Well, he's practically broke."

But Edgar Longstreet was far from broke and hog bellies were far from "bottoming out." Concealing his wealth, denying it, squirreling it away so it couldn't be taken from him, was innate in his nature, extending even to his wife who would be sure to find ways of wasting expendable income if she knew it was available.

Only Edgar and his accountant knew his true worth. Fran perceived the hog belly business as barely keeping afloat, and lived in fear of it sinking entirely, an event she tried hard not to dwell on.

During their twenty years of marriage Edgar had always made it clear that his clients came first. Fran understood the necessity of the large expenditures that came up from time to time, like $900 golf clubs to impress clients who could easily go elsewhere to buy hog bellies. She understood why Edgar had to have a new Mercedes every two or three years and keep it safe from vandals in a $300 a month garage in The City during working hours. And of course clients had to be continually wined and dined to stay impressed.

Fran understood all this and more. She pitied poor Edgar, enduring those three hour lunches in the finest restaurants, day in and day out, wooing new clients and indulging the old. A spartan lunch, leftovers from the refrigerator, satisfied her.

Sometimes she fantasized about Poverty Road and what it would be like to actually live there, should it ever come to that. She saw herself huddled in a crumbling tenement, and Edgar had died or was far away, and no children were there to comfort her. She was alone, because the time had never been right to bring children into the world. Edgar had always said it just wasn't feasible to have children when things were so bad.

But when such gloomy thoughts occurred to Fran she told herself, Don't think about that! Just don't think about it!

One day Fran succumbed to an impulse to take the bus to the City. The weather was perfect for window shopping, and later she would drop in on Edgar. She had rarely been to his office and fondly imagined the look of pleased surprise on his face when she walked in.

But when she arrived around two-thirty Edgar was still out to lunch and only the accountant was in the two-man office. He gave her a cup of coffee and they chatted awhile, he in Edgar's chair with his feet on Edgar's desk, she sitting in the client's chair.

Small talk was running out when Fran ventured to say, "I guess business is pretty bad these days, isn't it?"

The accountant laughed. "You're kidding, of course! Why, if it gets any better ... well, we'll just have to open our own bank."

Fran smiled, although she thought it a rather grim joke. "Open our own bank? Now who's kidding?"

"Oh sure. I was just trying to be funny. I only meant that business has been great all along, but right now it's nothing but terrific."

Fran looked closely at the accountant's smiling face, wondering if he was still trying to be funny. If not, then he was obviously unaware of the impact of his words: "business has been great ... right now it's nothing but terrific." She put her coffee cup down. Her hand was shaking.

She managed to return the accountant's smile. "Oh, I was just thinking about something Edgar said. It's nothing, really. I get things mixed up sometimes. I suppose that's why he calls me 'Vera Vague.'"

"Well, 'Vera,' don't bother your head about whatever it is. Edgar worries too much. He *invents* things to worry about. Listen, if anybody can keep Uncle Sam's greedy hands off the bottom line it's your husband." He laughed wholeheartedly, and Fran tried to rearrange her smile into a naive look.

"Is that what 'bottoming out' means?"

"Oh, Fran, you're so funny!" The accountant rewarded her wit with another laugh, an indulgent one. "You can be sure old Edgar will never bottom out. He'll never lose a dime as long as banks have safe deposit boxes, that's for sure. He's not piling up all that cash for the Uncle's business."

"I've never paid much attention, I'm afraid. How does it work?"

"Well, in the real world, Fran, it's just a matter of creative accounting. Dry stuff. You wouldn't be interested."

Fran looked at the tin watch she wore. I got it at Sears, she thought numbly. "Gosh! I've got to catch a bus," she said. "Well, thanks for the coffee. It's been nice talking to you. Tell Edgar I dropped in, won't you?"

Fran stared blindly out the bus window. So Edgar had been deceiving her all these years! Her face burned with anger and resentment. How could she have been so gullible, saving pennies, falling for that hard-up-hog- belly-broker routine? And now it turns out that he's actually a hog- belly-tycoon!

Walking home from the bus stop she computed the odds. Confront him? What good would that do now? See a lawyer? Maybe, but knowing Edgar, he'd get a better one and she'd live on a pittance the rest of her life. Not that she wasn't used to living on a pittance.

No. The best thing was to let it go, but revenge herself in other ways. Like make him spend money. He'd hate that.

There'll be some changes made, she thought, slipping her key into the lock. For one thing, no more nightmares about Poverty Road. And no more worry about bottoming out. The first shock was wearing off but her anger was building; betrayal and humiliation brought hot tears to her eyes and she wiped them away impatiently. I can't go on just feeling sorry for myself, she thought. I'll *do* something. I don't know what, but I'll *do* something.

Edgar leaned over the liquor cabinet after a late Sunday morning breakfast, rummaging for the makings of elevenses, his long body folded in half to search the bottom shelf.

Fran watched him from where she sat on the sofa, thinking that he was much the same as when she first met him twenty years before: two-thirds loosely jointed legs, like an oversize marionette; hair still the color of damp straw. He wasn't a hog-belly-baron then. "Big E" his friends had called him. How about calling him "Big L" for "Big Liar". He's the biggest liar ever. He's world class.

"Edgar," she said, "I want a piano."

"Where's that Red Label, Fran? It was here last night."

"You drank it. I want a piano, Edgar."

"Ah, here's an Old Overholt, practically full. Good Old Overshoes, that's what we used to call it. Get a couple of glasses, will you, hon?"

Fran's hands were folded in her lap, her feet neatly together. She didn't stir. "I want a piano, Edgar," she repeated.

Edgar gave her a dubious look, shrugged, and went to the kitchen. He came back waving a glass invitingly. "Want one, pet?"

"No. I want a piano."

Edgar splashed a dollop of water over two jiggers of Old Overshoes. He took a tentative gulp. His thinking was a little slow from last night's Red Label. The whiskey gave his brain a jolt, enabling him to receive and process outside information. Something about a piano. Something odd about the way his wife was sitting there watching him.

He mused, looking into his glass, then stared at the wall behind the sofa. His eyes glazed over.

"A pi-*an*-o." He mouthed the word as if it were the most bizarre noun in the language, stressing the second vowel. He said it again in the form of a question, "A pi-*an*-o? Sure you don't want a drink, hon?"

"You know what a piano is, don't you Edgar? A big thing with black and white keys? To play music on?"

"You don't need to be sarcastic, pet. Since you can't play a pi-*an*-o, I'm just wondering why you want one."

"I intend to take lessons."

"Honest to God, Fran, may I ask what brought this on? You must be losing your marbles or something. How much do you think a piano would cost me? Plus lessons? My God, only a mint, that's all!"

"You can afford it," Fran said. "And what I want is a baby grand, not some beat-up old secondhand upright."

Edgar freshened his drink. "Well, is that so, Fran? And I can afford it? That's news to me. Haven't I been telling you the market is liable to bottom out any day? Don't you ever listen? Don't you realize we're practically on Poverty Road?"

Fran dismissed Poverty Road with a casual wave. "Oh, you worry too much. Your accountant says you invent things to worry about."

Edgar nodded. "That's right, you talked to him the other day, didn't you?" He crossed the room and sat next to his wife on the sofa. "What else did he say about me?" He reached for her hand and she snatched it away.

"Nothing. We just talked about the weather, and since you weren't there I left. Edgar, *you're* going to buy *me* a piano."

Edgar went to the liquor cabinet to pick up his glass. He gazed into it, pondering. Fran's eyes never left his face. With her new perception of him as hog-belly-tycoon she could tell fairly accurately what was going on in his head: he was worried about her chat with the accountant; he was working on an incontestable anti-piano scheme; he was surprised that she hadn't caved in at the mention of Poverty Road.

"Now listen, hon," he began as if genuinely perplexed, "you know I'd buy you anything in the world if I could. But like I've told you over and over the market's down to zilch, nada, zero. I simply can't buy a piano right now or in the near future. I don't have the money."

Fran said, "Is that a fact, now."

"It sure is." He swung his head sadly from side to side about the way things stood hog-bellywise. Fran stared at him without a flicker of sympathy as he produced a gusty sigh and after a thoughtful moment, brightened up with sudden inspiration.

"Hey! Tell you what, pet! I've got an idea! How about renting an accordion? I bet you'd like that. You could carry it around, play it at parties if you wanted to. A piano just sits there, taking up space. What d'you say, hon? Isn't that a great idea?"

"An accordion?" Fran's stiff back went limp on the sofa. "To play at parties? What parties? When was the last time we were invited to a party?" She closed her eyes and shook her head.

Edgar had played his ace with mention of Poverty Road. His always amenable wife had slumped down and closed her eyes. He went in for the kill.

"Remember when you wanted to be an artist, pet? All that paint and stuff cost me an arm and a leg and it's all dried up and blown away. And remember when you went back to school, to finish your education, I think you said? That didn't last long, did it? You bought enough books to start a library, and they weren't cheap. God, Fran, the truth is, you just don't stick to things."

Without opening her eyes Fran said, "I went two semesters. I got all A's." But she wasn't up to debating old issues. "Oh never mind all that." She stood. "My head is aching. I want to lie down."

On Monday Frances Longstreet called Sherman & Clay to inquire about renting an accordion that she probably wouldn't stick with or take to parties. But she would practice! The moment she heard Edgar's car in the garage she would start. He couldn't complain. It was his great idea. All smiles, she would ask, "How am I doing, Edgar?" and tell him she had to practice scales fifty times a day before she could even *think* of learning to play a melody. "I've only done ten so far today," she would say. "Oh your dinner's in the oven, such as it is. I've got to catch up on my practicing."

She had canceled the viable options of seeing a lawyer and/or confronting Edgar as too late and too much hassle. Maybe, after all, the accountant had been joking. He certainly had laughed a lot. Maybe he was being ironic and she was too dumb to understand that it was supposed to be funny. So what? She just didn't care anymore.

But rich or poor, Edgar owed her something for years of going without ordinary things most wives took for granted, like nice clothes and being able to accept and reciprocate invitations. And most of all — if the accountant was right — for day after day and in her dreams at night, for living in the

37

shadow of Poverty Road. One way or another, Fran was going to get back at least some of her lost self-esteem, starting with this rented pile of reeds and bellows.

Edgar's Mercedes pulled into the garage and she harnessed herself into the unwieldy instrument.

"Practice, practice, practice!" she murmured. "Practice makes perfect, they say."

Smith of the Burning Eyes and Edith

The canine population of Cardinal Court increased by about two and a half pounds when Smith and Edith and her chihuahua came to live at Number 16. The previous owners, Harvey and Debbie, were moving "upscale." Harvey's star had risen in his "major corporation," and he required a more prestigious address.

On moving-out day Harvey stood on the sidewalk instructing the indifferent moving-men in the art of moving furniture. Marianne Fallon and other ladies of the court came by for the seeing-off, providing Harvey with an audience to entertain with details of his new home in Redtail Hawk Hill.

"It's got just about everything," he told the ladies. "Completely fenced in. Nobody gets in — or out either, for that matter — except bona fide homeowners. We've all got one of those plastic cards, see, to open the gates. Electronic, I mean. I guess Redtail Hawk Hill is pretty exclusive, if you know what I mean."

Marianne Fallon nodded. She knew exactly what he meant. She had tried often and unsuccessfully to promote just such cards for Cardinal Court, along with speed bumps and twenty-four hour security guards. And no children under eighteen. (Dogs were okay.)

39

Debbie came from the house laden with treasures too precious for the rough hands of moving-men. In jeans and T-shirt, her dark hair pulled back in a ponytail, she looked younger than her twenty-eight or so years. Her cheeks dimpled in a smug smile. This was her big moment, a chance to snub Marianne and her nosy friends for snubbing her because … well … just because.

"Did Harvey tell you we've got four bathrooms? And three fireplaces, one in the back yard? And there's a four-car garage, too. It's a *really* big house, but of course we *need* a big house for entertaining." She went on, relishing the emphasis she managed to put on just about every other word, "Harvey and I expect to do a *lot* of entertaining at Redtail. That's what *we* all call it, Redtail. We've met so *many,* such awfully *nice* people there, and I can *tell* they really *like* me, they're so *friendly* and all."

The ladies got the two-part message as clearly as though Debbie had spoken the words aloud: (a) All residents of Redtail and all guests *chez* Harvey and Debbie were naturally light years superior to the likes of them, and (b) So who needs you, you nosy old prudes — eat your hearts out in your dinky little houses and see if I care.

Harvey was saying, "Listen, you've all got to come and see us when we're settled, okay? Let's keep in touch, right?"

Gen McMurdo murmured to Joannie Dettner, "Hey! That'll be the day. As if we ever see hide nor hair of *him* again." Joannie giggled. "Did she say *Rat* Tail Hill, or am I hearing things?" And Maggie Watson whispered, "That fence will sure cramp Debbie's style but maybe her boyfriends can scale it." Marianne Fallon whispered "Shush! Stop that whispering!" and to Harvey she said, "Oh, it sounds just marvelous! I'd love to see it. We all would. Just let us know when you're ready to give us the grand tour." She looked coolly at Debbie. "I do hope you'll be happy there, dear."

"Oh, I'm *sure* I will, Marianne. Like I said, everyone's so *nice* there."

The movers were closing up the van. The time had come for Harvey and Debbie to shake off the dust of Cardinal Court forever. Driving off in their separate cars they waved and called, "Goodbye! Goodbye!" But the voice that called, "Don't forget now, you're coming to see us soon! Keep in touch!" was not Debbie's.

Gazing at the now empty Number 16, Marianne Fallon said, "I wonder what the Smiths will be like.

The Smiths turned out to be an unremarkable couple in their fifties. (But that was only a first impression, often deceptive.) The furniture going in passed muster. Some pieces were even admired by dog-walking ladies. But that Chihuahua! Wasn't that a sad excuse for a dog? Marianne Fallon's Doberman pincher mistook the little beast for a large rat and tried to eat it.

"Why, I had to hold on to the leash for dear life to keep Cookie from chewing the poor little thing to pieces. Thank God nobody was around," Marianne told the ladies.

Lottie Dixon, next door to the Smiths at Number 18, reported that *he* was red-faced, heavy-set, no neck, ex-football type. *She* was small, you might even say tiny, sort of vague looking, and her clothes looked expensive.

On a foggy night Mona Lisa and Gunlak Johansen were walking the bulldog, Sven Two, when out of the darkness and into the misty glow of a street light, tiny unremarkable Edith

Smith materialized; then the Chihuahua, Precious, appeared at the far end of a very long leash.

Edith was singing,

> "I may be wrong BUT
> I think you're WONderful,
> Just WONderful, my dear,"

and, she was as naked as her little dog. The Johansens smiled and nodded, wished her a pleasant "Good evening!" and went on their way. At a safe distance they broke into laughter.

"Oh, my God! Can you believe it?" Mona Lisa gasped. "Nothing! Not a stitch on! And not a bit concerned!" She grabbed Gunlak's arm to keep from collapsing with mirth.

Gunlak shouted out, "Bare-assed! Like a peeled banana! What a woman!"

"And singing!" Mona Lisa yelled.

"Let's take up a collection, folks. Buy her a medal," Gunlak called into the foggy night. "It's got to be a first! Around here, anyway. Right, neighbors?"

Mona Lisa choked back her laughter. "Yes! A medal! But how could you pin it on her bare chest?"

The next Edith-in-the-nude sighting occurred in broad daylight. Lottie Dixon, pulling into her garage, observed Edith sashaying along, wearing nothing at all and dragging Precious half a block behind. She was singing,

> "By the time I get to Phoenix
> He'll be waking. OH YEAH!"

Lottie clapped her hands over her astonished open mouth. Oh, just look at her, she thought. She's so frail! And singing like that. I ought to do something. She's got a screw loose or something. I better call Gen or Marianne. Oh, the poor little thing!

Then she saw Smith in her rearview mirror. He was partially concealed behind a rhododendron bush. She heard a "Psst!" and a plea, "Edith, please! Come in, will you? Edith? Come on now, Edith!"

Edith flipped him a casual wave and segued smoothly into,

> "I'm goin' to Jackson, YEAH, YEAH,
> I'm goin' to Jackson, WATCH OUT!"

This happened to be the afternoon preceding the night that Smith was throwing a party to welcome himself to Cardinal Court. Everyone was invited, and anxious to see what, if anything, Edith would be wearing, everyone accepted. Word of her penchant for nudity had spread.

Edith was fully clothed in billowing mu-mu and wore a demure smile. Precious was not to be seen. He was hiding under a kitchen sink, having seen that certain look in Smith's eyes before; that burning gleam spelled trouble for small dogs.

Smith loved parties and this would be his first with his new neighbors. He liked to get a party off to a good start by doubling the gin in the martini pitcher and refilling the glasses before they were half empty. Guests sometimes thought they were still on their first one until too late.

Number 16 soon rocked with revelry. A collection of Swing provided the impetus for singing and dancing, and some Cardinal Court residents were rumored to be "fooling around in the kitchen." Marianne Fallon put in an appearance and quickly left, clucking her tongue. A few timid ladies followed suit.

When somebody dropped a tray of cheesepuffs at the same moment the martini pitcher crashed to the hearth, Smith abandoned the niceties of ice cubes and olives, vermouth and glasses, and offered plain gin, to be drunk from the neck of the bottle.

Smith's eyes burned over the quart of Beefeater when he lifted it to his lips and glimpsed a number of his guests tottering toward home via the front door.

"Don't go!" he begged, shouting at them. "Hang around! The night's young and the party's just getting started!"

Gen McMurdo almost made it to the door, but Smith barred her way. She sank down woozily on a sofa.

"Gen!" Smith cried, "are you okay? I've got to tell you something, Gen! I love you!"

Smith really did love Gen at that moment. He loved her hour-glass figure, her deep bosom, and where most of the hour-glass sand had settled, her round bottom. He tried to pry the Beefeater between her lips and clenched teeth, his eyes burning above her scowling face.

"C'mon, Gen, let's have a drink. I love you, Gen."

Gen swatted at the bottle with her limp hand. "Oh, for God's sake, Smith, knock it off, will you?"

Glancing up, he saw Edith dancing solo and slipping out of her mu-mu. She was singing along with a record on the turntable,

> "I don't want to set the world on FI-re,
> I just want to BE the flame in your heart."

In one agile ex-football player leap Smith cleared the sofa and Gen's supine body. "Edith!" he yelled. "Please!" Edith was tossing her mu-mu out the door, out into the patio, out into the night.

"Oh to hell with it!" Smith shrugged. "I ought to put you away. And I would, too, if your old man wasn't almost dead and so damn rich."

He looked around the deserted living room. Where had everybody gone? Only Gen McMurdo was left, snoring on the sofa, and Edith, dancing in the buff and singing another old favorite,

> "The party's over old girl
> Take off your makeup it's over,
> All over, my friend."

The Smiths didn't abide long at Number 16. A few months after the party Edith's father died, leaving her heir to millions made in the rag trade. Ladies-ready-to-wear with the label "Miss Edith" sold in department stores all over the country.

Like Harvey and Debbie, the Smiths wanted a more prestigious address. Smith did, that is. Edith couldn't care less where she hung the clothes she threw off. Silverado was Smith's choice, a good place to mingle with other rich millionaires.

On moving-out day Smith mentioned to the ladies of the court who came to see him off, that he planned to throw a party to welcome himself to Silverado. Gen McMurdo, as a veteran of Smith's now famous party, tried to dissuade him.

"Oh, God, Smith, why don't you give those poor people a break? They're all old, aren't they? Silverado is for old people, isn't it? Why, you could kill them all off in one swoop with just one of your parties."

The irony of Edith's inheritance, the fortune made from the very clothes she shucked off at every opportunity, was not lost on the denizens of Cardinal Court. Mona Lisa and Gunlak Johansen, the first to run into Edith au natural, talked it over.

"Maybe as a child Daddy forced her to model the kiddie line and she developed a loathing of clothes," Mona Lisa suggested. Gunlak said, "Yeah, and maybe she was born with some major marbles missing." There had been other sporadic sightings of Edith bare, and Gunlak said he was sorry to see her leave. "That little naked songbird added a little spice to this place. You gotta admit it's strictly from Dullsville, right?"

Some time after the Smiths had gone, Joannie Dettner heard the sequel to their story from a friend who played golf at Silverado. Edith didn't sing anymore. No one there had ever heard her repertoire of golden oldies. Nowadays she was always fully dressed, and as far as other millionaires knew, in her right mind. This friend said that even Precious wore a little overcoat on his daily walks.

Smith had given a very nice party, very circumspect; nothing untoward happened. Silveradoeans were offered drinks only from glasses. Edith passed the cheesepuffs in a dignified manner, and guests discussed the terrible conditions of the country, the low rate of interest on bonds and the threat of higher income taxes. Things like that.

"No wonder she doesn't sing anymore," Joannie Dettner said, "Not much to sing about. And I bet Smith's got her in therapy or something."

Gen McMurdo said, "I suppose at an affair like that Smith wasn't making too many passes at the ladies. I'm sorry in a way. It would be a shame to break the spirit behind those burning eyes."

"I guess it's true that money changes people," Maggie Watson said, "but unless I win the lottery I'll never know for sure."

A Time for Daffodils

M aggie Watson's husband left her on a Sunday afternoon in October, the day they planted the daffodils. Kneeling at his side, digging little holes for the bulbs, Maggie said, "I love planting daffodils. It always makes me think of how nice it will be when they come up in February. February is the best month of all, don't you think so too, Walter?"

"Sure, I guess so." Walter dropped the last bulb into its pre-dug hole.

"Well, for me it is, anyway," Maggie went on. "I love it when the acacia blooms almost overnight on the hills, and daffodils poke up all of a sudden. I'm always surprised, like I didn't expect it to happen so soon."

Walter stood, brushing soil and planting mix from his knees. He looked past her, at the top of the fence where a drab brown bird hopped and pecked. "I won't be here to see them bloom, Maggie."

Maggie tamped down the earth around the bulbs and wiped her hands on her jeans. "Oh? Is the firm sending you to L.A. in February?" she asked without much interest. "Gosh, they really plan ahead, don't they?"

Walter raised his eyes to the bright autumn sky, searching for inspiration, then lowered his gaze to a point just beyond his wife's left shoulder. He sighed expelling a little puff of air, that sounded like "Whew!" Subtlety never had worked with Maggie. "I mean ... " he said, articulating each word slowly and clearly, "I mean I'm leaving you, Maggie. I mean I don't want to be married to you any more."

Kneeling, Maggie looked up at him in open mouthed astonishment. He couldn't have said that, she thought. Not my Walter. No!

But her Walter was already walking away, down the path to the house. She heard the kitchen door open and slam shut. Then the garage door went up and she heard his car start up and drive off. The garage door closed itself.

Four days after Walter's defection, the Cardinal Court Ladies Thursday Morning Koffee Klatch met at Lottie Dixon's house. Maggie arrived with red swollen eyes. Lottie hugged her tenderly. "Oh my God, Mag! I heard the news! Come on in! You look ghastly, just standing there like that, like one of the walking wounded!"

Maggie sobbed, "He left me, Lottie. He said he didn't want to be married to me any more. He just up and left me! Just like that!"

Marianne Fallon and Joannie Dettner came from the kitchen with the coffee and Danish. Gen McMurdo followed with cups and plates. Lottie sat Maggie in a chair and the others came to hover over her, chorusing soothing words. "Don't cry, honey ... He's not worth it ... We're all here for you ... We all love you, Mag ..."

Gen McMurdo stage whispered to Joannie Dettner, "That jerk, Walter! I could kill him! I never liked him anyway. Old Silent Sam."

"Me neither." Joannie shook her head. "Still waters and all that stuff. You can't trust them as far as you can throw them."

Marianne Fallon waved a schoolteacherly index finger. "Shut up, both of you. That kind of talk won't help Maggie a bit."

Lottie bent over Maggie, taking her hand. "Now listen, honey, you've just got to stop all this crying and *do* something. Like get a lawyer, for instance. I'll bet *he's* got one already."

Maggie wailed, "I don't want a lawyer! I want my Walter back! I miss him. I know what you all think of him, but he's just naturally quiet, that's all. Some people are *like* that, you know."

The ladies looked at one another, rolled their eyes and shrugged. Maggie really liked this guy who never opened his mouth. They filled their coffee cups and dispersed comfortably around the room. Lottie Dixon asked, "How long were you and Walter married, Mag? Years and years, wasn't it?"

"Twelve years. We were married *twelve* years. I used to try to draw him out, try to get him to express himself, but I gave that up. So he wasn't a terrific conversationalist. So what? I kind of *intuited* things, know what I mean? Only now ... I guess I wasn't as good a mind reader as I thought I was, was I?"

In her eagerness to explain her feelings for Walter, Maggie's tears had dried. Encouraged by the support of the ladies she smiled bravely. "I feel better now. You're good friends and I thank you all for caring about me."

"Know what I think, Maggie?" Gen McMurdo asked. The ladies, afraid that Gen was about to blurt out what they all secretly thought, sent scathing looks in her direction. Gen failed to notice. "I think your Walter is having a mid-life crisis. I'll bet he thinks he's missed something. Maybe he's found himself another woman and maybe he's chatting it up with her right now because he's decided he's got something to say after all. It happens all the time. They just take off. The woods are full of them." Hanging on to Gen's words, Maggie resumed weeping.

"Gen! How can you be so cruel!" Marianne Fallon exclaimed. "I wish you'd learn to keep your own mouth shut once in a while. Now you've got her crying again!"

Gen said, "I'm sorry Mag, but you've got to face facts. Your darling Walter was not a real sweet guy when he walked away and left you kneeling in the dirt. Doesn't that tell you he had other plans for himself?"

Lottie Dixon put a protective arm around Maggie's shoulder. "Why can't you give the poor girl a break, Gen? Can't you see how hard you're making it for her?" Gen shrugged and bit into a Danish.

Joannie Dettner said, "You didn't tell us what you said when he said he didn't want to be married to you any more. What on Earth did you say, Maggie?"

Maggie sighed and sniffled. "I guess I didn't say anything. I must have been in shock because I couldn't believe my ears." And glaring at Gen McMurdo she added, "You didn't know Walter at all, and I don't care what you say about him. You always act like you know everything, and you don't."

The Koffee Klatch broke up with Maggie the recipient of loving words and pats and thoughtful remarks about the well-documented ability of time to heal all wounds.

Some weeks later forlorn Maggie's turn to host the Koffee Klatch came around. When all were present Marianne Fallon called for attention, clanking her coffee cup with a spoon. "Listen everybody — especially you Mag — wait till you hear this! It's not good news, but I'm sure it's much better for Maggie to hear it from me, among us friends. It's this … well … yesterday I was in Nordie's and …"

Maggie wailed in anticipation of the not good news. Her tears flowed. Gen McMurdo gave her a sour look. "Oh for God's sake quit that sniveling. We all want to hear what happened yesterday at Nordie's. Marianne seems to think it's earth shaking."

"Okay, Gen, that's enough." Marianne started again. "Well, yesterday, who did I see but that waitress … you know … from Joe's Place? She walks knock-kneed and pigeon-toed so her fanny will wiggle? The one with the big boobs?"

"Hey, I thought you said this was about Nordie's," Joannie interrupted. "Now it's Joe's Place."

"I'm *getting* to that part! Will you kindly hold your horses?"

"Well," Joannie was stung and answered caustically, "if there's a point to this story just get to it. Yes, we know the waitress and yes, we know how she walks and we know how big her boobs are. So, what else happened yesterday?"

Exasperated, Marianne raised her voice. "Oh! I'm trying to tell you! If you'd just listen! I saw *her* with *him*. Walter, I mean. Yes! Walter! Upstairs in the Petites. She had on this short, tight dress — none of us would be found dead in it, Mag — and she was bouncing around, modeling it for him. This was at *Nordie's*, Joannie, not Joe's Place."

Joannie Dettner laughed. "Boy! She'd make a good model at that. Plenty of practice in that knock-kneed pigeon-toed way of walking." Marianne ignored the remark and was about to go on when Maggie screamed, "It wasn't Walter! I don't believe you! Walter never even notices clothes!"

"Why should I make up such a thing, Mag, I *saw* them.

Whispering together and laughing. Real palsy-walsy, if you know what I mean."

"Aha! So I was right, wasn't I!" Gen McMurdo grinned in triumph. "I told you so! And you said I was cruel."

This new development was thoroughly discussed until the Koffee Klatch ended. Maggie was left to do the cleanup and some serious crying. She also did some serious thinking.

Maggie's serious thinking got her as far as the Petites at Nordstrom where she lurked between the racks on the off chance of spotting Walter buying clothes for the knock-kneed waitress. No such luck, but one day in a nearby coffee shop she met Mona Lisa. Maggie knew she was supposed to snub Mona Lisa because the other ladies snubbed her and she was bound in sisterhood. But Mona Lisa was warm and likable, and quite willing to listen to her sad story. Telling it to a fresh audience was surprisingly exhilarating. Mona Lisa invited Maggie to come home with her for a drink, and thrilled with her sympathetic new friend, Maggie was happy to accept.

Mona Lisa's furniture was not "tacky" as the ladies had led Maggie to believe. On the contrary, it was quite lovely. "You should have seen the god-awful junk I rented when I first moved here," Mona Lisa told her. "My own furniture took months to arrive from Mallorca."

"Oh? Is that so? Then I guess that's why ... " Maggie stopped short of explaining why the ladies had concluded that Mona Lisa and her chattels were unworthy of neighborhood standards.

Mona Lisa laughed. "I think I know what you were going to say. Some of our neighbors took that rented stuff as a personal affront. I know that now, but don't worry, I can live without them. Do you know Jessie Donley and Kate Kardis? They've been wonderful friends. Except for you, now, Maggie, they're my only friends in Cardinal Court."

Maggie acknowledged with a nod that she knew Jessie and Kate. Shame kept her from speaking. She sipped the ice-cold vodka Mona Lisa offered her, something she thought only Russians drank.

Mona Lisa said, "I don't suppose you know I got married? Since I moved here last Fall? Let me tell you about my great romance! I married the man who delivered my furniture!" Maggie laughed, pleased to discover that she still knew how.

"You'll meet Gunlak and we'll tell you all about the wedding. A censored version, I'm afraid. It was pretty hectic. He should be home soon. You'll like him, Maggie, he's fun and you need cheering up."

Gunlak arrived home with his friend and furniture-moving buddy, Olaf Neilsen, an unexpected but welcome dinner guest.

Maggie stayed for dinner, too. Gunlak tossed salad, singing his theme song, "Get Me to the Church on Time" in his vibrant baritone. Olaf poured more vodka. Mona Lisa broiled steaks and Maggie set the table.

She liked the easygoing ways of these ebullient Swedes, different from an impression she had picked up somewhere that Swedes were a somber and phlegmatic lot. Not so, she thought now. Walter is Scotch or something and he hardly ever laughed. Swedes laugh a lot.

The gay dinner party was positively boisterous in the opinion of the circumspect Maggie who loved every minute of it. Her new friends ate, danced and sang simultaneously. And Olaf, especially, teased her as though they were old and familiar friends.

Maggie had a wonderful time. and when at the party's end Olaf asked her if she'd like to see a movie with him sometime, "or whatever," she looked to Mona Lisa for approval. Smiling, Mona Lisa nodded Yes, but whispered in Gunlak's ear, "He's not married or anything, is he?" "He was. Not now," Gunlak whispered back. "Hey! Don't worry! Olaf's a great guy. He's a Swede, isn't he? Like me, you lucky girl!"

Without the knowledge and consent of the ladies of the court the romance of Maggie and Olaf flourished. At a Koffee Klatch on Thursday morning Gen McMurdo remarked, "How come you're so cheerful these days, Mag? Don't tell me dear Walter has had a change of heart?"

"I've noticed something different about you, too, Maggie," Marianne Fallon said. "Are you and Walter getting together again?" Maggie Watson gazed at her curious friends in wide-eyed innocence. "Walter? ... Walter who?" she asked.

The daffodils Maggie and Walter had planted in October came up in February on schedule. Maggie and Olaf were married against a background of yellow blooms. Mona Lisa and Gunlak Johansen were matron of honor and best man, and the only guests at the simple ceremony. The bride carried a bouquet of the sunny, home grown daffodils.

The "Company Picnic"

Kate Kardis had picked up a dozen stuffed eggs at the deli as Jessie Donley's contribution to the Homeowners Annual Labor Day Picnic, and on her own threw in a jar of pickles and a can of olives. She carried these donations down the flagstone steps to the pool and put them on the trestle table set up for the occasion.

The busy ladies of the picnic committee ignored her, but she greeted them cheerfully. "Good morning, girls," she said. That was bound to get their hackles up. Too familiar. The ladies didn't deign to answer and Kate left, climbing up the flagstone steps, smiling to herself.

Marianne Fallon remarked, intending to be overheard, "And just how are we supposed to open that can, with our teeth? Of course it wouldn't occur to *her* to open it, would it? Or bring a can opener and a bowl or something to put them in."

Kate thought, so they did notice me. Well, well. So I'm not quite invisible after all. Her smile widened.

The ladies of the court resented Kate because of her friendship with Jessie Donley. Jessie pretended not to hear her doorbell when they called on her individually or as a group, while Kate had entrée any time she rang. And worst of all, she tied those dumb dogs of hers to Jessie's mailbox post, just so they'd know she was inside and they were out.

At the top of the steps Kate said to herself, wouldn't they be surprised to hear Jessie say They can ring till their thumbs fall off. I'm retired, Kate, and I won't endure those women. They bore me stiff.

Cardinal Court homeowners held an undivided interest in the swimming pool and common areas, and all could attend the annual picnic, even those Marianne Fallon didn't like. Those people, she said, who were never seen all year round but showed up on Labor Day with a bevy of strangers in tow, relatives and such. And of course the strangers never brought so much as a peanut butter sandwich. But they weren't shy, were they, about bellying up to the bar and eating everything in sight! It made her furious, she said. Simply furious.

Tilting her head to one side to enjoy the effect of the garnish of sliced radishes with which she had improved some homeowner's potato salad, Marianne pondered aloud. "H'mmm … not too bad … quite nice, in fact … a few olives wouldn't hurt … if we could get *her* stupid can open."

She gave the food laid out on the table a final check. "I guess we're about ready, everybody. Let's go powder our noses before the hordes descend."

Marianne's suggestions were usually construed as commands, so the picnic committee trotted off to powder their noses.

Year after year the Labor Day picnic followed a predictable course, as if it had all been laid out long ago and nothing would ever change it. Someone would drink too much and fall in the pond fully clothed; someone would suffer hurt feelings and cry; Gen McMurdo would dance the hula-hula. And so on. But this year would be different. One homeowner would not survive the day.

Before noon the picnickers began to trickle down the flagstone steps to stake a claim on an umbrella table, a lounge, a spot on the grass. "Those people" Marianne Fallon didn't like were busy identifying themselves to the "regular people" who pretended to remember them from previous picnics, falsely explaining, "Oh yes! Good to see you! How are you? Been a while, hasn't it?"

The householders, gathered together for a yearly fun time, had to get used to mixing before they could relax. Polite and cool at first, it wasn't until shy Lottie Dixon broke the ice with her abrupt arrival on the scene that their circumspect behavior evaporated.

Coming down the hill Lottie missed the first step and didn't manage to find the second, the third, or any other step at all. She bounced and tumbled down to land sitting on the grass, a surprised look on her face. The prim little Miss Lottie let out a terrible shriek, then uncharacteristically screamed, "Goddamn it to hell!" Her shocked close friends gasped. But later they speculated privately that Lottie must have worked up courage to join the fun with the help of the cooking sherry and OD'd on it.

The picnickers burst into tension-relieving laughter. Lottie's comic pratfall did the trick, the party warmed up. The afternoon wore on, the buffet was demolished, the bar several times replenished. The sun declined and the moon rose. Conviviality was rampant. Laughter resonated on the soft September air and moonbeams danced on the water as revelers splashed and shoved one another into the pool.

At the peak of the festivities Gen McMurdo swung into her Hawaiian number. Barefoot and grass skirted, paper leis falling on her bosom, paper flowers wreathing her brow, she strummed her ukelele. Like the ebb and flow of ocean waves, she swayed and writhed to an ancient rhythm, singing of nut-brown maidens, little grass shacks and little fishies that go nuka-nuka huka huka swimming by.

The trouble with Gen McMurdo's song and dance act was that she didn't know when to quit. The fans grew restless, hearing her songs repeated again and again, losing their first enthusiasm for her non-stop undulating hips, and the tuneless strumming of the ukelele got on their nerves.

By mutual consent, the picnickers acted out a favorite Labor Day ritual: the flinging of Gen McMurdo, paper flowers, grass skirt, ukelele, all and everything, songs and singer, into the pool.

Jessie Donley and Kate Kardis elected to sit out the picnic on Jessie's deck. Behind woody hydrangea bushes that screened them in, they could view the goings-on below without being seen themselves.

Kate said it sure beats actually being there by a mile, and Jessie said wild horses couldn't drag her down there. She said it reminded her of those deadly company picnics she and Ed were obliged to go to before he got his appointment and they went to Washington.

"Oh Lord," Jessie reminisced, "I'll never forget those miserable affairs. One time these huge hairy caterpillars kept falling out of a tree and crawling in my hair. Oh, it was just awful! I couldn't stop screaming! Ed picked them out one at a time and stepped on them. Ugh!"

Kate smiled at the story, but something about the way Jessie had slumped down in her chair began to worry her. *Something's wrong,* she thought, *she doesn't look well. Maybe she's just tired today. Oh, God, I hope she's not getting sick!*

Jessie was a "fine figure of a woman," tall and stately, while Kate was small and wispy-thin, almost childlike in appearance. She was a decade younger than Jessie, but still felt like a big sister whose job it was to take care of a little sister.

"Oh sure! Tell me about those picnics, Jess!" She laughed, hiding her concern. "I've been there too, y'know. Ants and bees and bugs! Bees are the worst of all. You'd be eating something and a bee would land on it. Imagine if you bit into a bee! Imagine if you swallowed one and it stung your insides!"

Jessie reached for the glass next to her chair. It was early afternoon but she and Kate didn't wait for the sun to go down on holidays like Labor Day. She sipped her drink, her eyes bright with recollection over the rim of the glass.

"Picnics always had to be on the hottest day of the year, didn't they, Kate? I think it was an unwritten rule. A test to see how much bacteria all that food could collect by sitting in the hot sun. I could never eat a bite, thinking of salmonella." Jessie shuddered dramatically and Kate laughed.

"Tell you what, Jess. Right here there's not a caterpillar, not a bug, not a bee in sight. A fly might show up, but if it does I'll zap it! So let's have a bugless company picnic, just you and I on the deck watching the entertainment at the pool. I'll get the binoculars."

"I'm afraid I neglected to make potato salad this morning, Kate. You can't have a picnic without potato salad."

"Well, I just happened to swipe two of your stuffed eggs, Jess, and as along as I just happened to be in the deli I got two ham and swiss on rye. We'll make do with what we have."

"Yeah, but *they* got the pickles and olives. I hope you didn't bring a can opener?"

"Of course not. I wouldn't dream of it. Me, miss a chance like that to bug your friend Marianne Fallon? Never!"

Jessie grinned, but in Kate's eyes seemed somehow slowed down. And paler than an hour ago. Oh, God, she thought, maybe she *is* sick. Not just tired.

But Jessie pulled herself up straighter in her chair and appeared to be perking up a bit. She said, "Fine. So on with our exclusive company picnic, Kate. You get the Old Crow and bring it out here. And a pitcher of water and some ice. Watching our neighbors frolic could be a thirsty business. And oh yes, bring some paper napkins. You know where they are?"

"I do indeed, Madam Queen. I know the royal kitchen like the back of my hand." Kate got up, bowed, and walked backwards to the front door. "But first, oh Queenly One, I've got to take my dogs home. I can't let them stay tied up all day. Bad for morale. I'll feed them and let them loose in my backyard." She blew Jessie a kiss. "Be right back."

"Yes, do hurry back, Kate dear." Kate sensed an urgency in Jessie's voice that made her even more uneasy.

Jessie's binoculars, held by Kate, swept the scene at the pool. By now the moon had risen, and Kate reported, "Oh-oh! Gen's going up to get into her grass skirt." The area, brightly lighted by lamps timed to go on at dusk, revealed even more details than daylight.

"Now what d'ya know," Kate announced, "there's Maggie with her new husband. H'mm ... not bad. Here, take a look, Jess."

Jessie took the glasses briefly and handed them back. "Oh, they're too heavy for me, Kate. Just tell me what's going on. Tell me about Maggie. Did old whatshisname Watson drop dead or something?"

"Lord no, Jess! Walter's alive and kicking. He ran off with that waitress at Joe's Cafe. You know, the one that wiggles when she walks? Caused quite a stir at the coffee klatch, I hear. I thought I told you!"

"Not a word. That man! He never opens his mouth! How on earth did he pull something like *that* off?"

"It was love, Jessie. Love loosened his tongue, I guess. Anyway, Mona Lisa told me about it. The new husband's name is Olaf. He's Gunlak's assistant moving-man. Dumb Walter is history."

Jessie shook her head. "Maggie didn't waste much time, did she? I suppose she's a nonperson now, among the elite?"

"Yeah. Like me and Mona Lisa. But of course you're still a candidate for elitehood. Still in the running, anyway."

"Can I help it if I'm just lucky, Kate?"

Kate stood up and bowed. "May a nonperson get more ice, Your Majesty? And as long as she's in the kitchen, anything else Your Graciousness desires?"

"Nothing. Not a thing, my dear. Just go and come back."

Kate was gone only a few minutes, hurrying because the "and come back" part worried her. Could it mean "don't leave me"?

Jessie was lying back in her chair, slack and awkward looking when Kate returned. Her chin was tilted up and her mouth open. Her eyes were closed. As if desperately wanting Kate to believe that everything was quite normal, she murmured a question that sounded like, "Has Gen done the hula yet?"

Kate, hearing the slurred words, wanted to cry out, "Oh, God, what's wrong with you?" Instead, keeping up the pretense, she answered, "Not yet, Jessie. It's too early. She's standing in the wings waiting for the right moment, tuning up her uke."

Still with her eyes closed, Jessie said clearly, spacing the words, "If you don't mind ... Kate dear ... I think I'll ... lie down. Just for ... a while."

"Oh my God! Jessie, what's the matter? Please tell me!"

"I'm ... not ... well." A grimace of pain pantomimed her halting words. Her eyes opened and she tried to rise but slumped back. Her breath came in labored rasping gasps. Her face was ashen.

"Oh, Jessie!" Kate implored. "Please tell me what to do!"

Jessie was unresponsive. Kate raised her voice, almost screaming, "Listen to me! Try to put your arms around my neck ... I can lift you. I'll help you to your bed ... please try!"

Jessie's right hand fluttered feebly to her chest and fell in her lap.

The number was thumbtacked to the wall next to the telephone. Kate dialed and waited an eternity to hear the doctor's calm voice: "I'm sending an ambulance. It's on its way now. Don't do anything. Just stay with her and wait. I'll see you at Marin General. I'll find you there. Don't worry, I'll find you."

She sat on the deck holding her friend's hand, listening for the siren's wail. Laughter and cheering rose from below. Gen must be into her act, she thought. Oh Jessie, don't die. Please don't die.

Only a few diehards were still celebrating Labor Day at Cardinal Court's annual picnic when Jessie Donley's damaged heart stopped beating. The doctor found Kate as promised, in a visitor's room. "We did all we could, Mrs. Kardis. It wasn't enough. I'm sorry."

Kate said nothing, she only wanted him to go away, this man who failed to save Jessie's life.

"I'm afraid you've had a bad shock," he said. "Let me get someone to take you home." She shook her head. No. "Well," he hesitated, "if you're sure you'll be all right ..." He put a small envelope in her hand. "Take one of these when you get home. A mild sedative. It will help."

He left and Kate wrapped herself in her arms, rocking, holding tight to her grief.

Jessie's not dead! ... I won't have it! ... She wouldn't die right in the middle of our small company picnic ... I could tell she was tired ... that's all ... just tired ... people don't die because they're tired ... Oh my God my dogs! ... tied to her mailbox? ... No, no ... I took them home ... I remember that ... poor Jessie hated dogs.

The first tears came with the thought of her dogs. She wouldn't be tying Blossom and Twinkie to Jessie's mailbox again. Never again.

A Breath Away

The elite Thursday morning Koffee Klatch met at Lottie Dixon's a few days after Robert and Emily Grady moved into Number 24 Cardinal Court, once the late Jessie Donley's home. Of course the newcomers were the main topic that day, for discussion and dissection. The ladies of the court expressed disappointment, peeved because the Gradys had moved in "in the dark of night," as Gen McMurdo put it. This in itself stirred vibes of suspicion. And besides, it must be said, the late night arrival of the moving van cheated the ladies of their deserved and proper right to inspect the Grady household goods and chattels in the broad light of day, as was their custom while walking their dogs, their built-in excuse to check out new people.

Said goods and chattels were actually unloaded at Number 24 in the same time frame as Prime Time TV, when the ladies were enjoying favorite sitcoms, deaf to the rumblings of the van pulling and hauling into the driveway.

"I never heard one single thing, did any of you?" Maggie Neilsen admitted. Hairdos shook from side to side in silent chorus: Nope. Nor I. Me neither. Nary a soul had heard one single thing.

Gen McMurdo said in her know-it-all way, "If you ask me, I'd say there's something pretty fishy about waiting till dark to show up with a truckful of stuff. Y'know what *I* think ... ?"

"Oh sure, Gen. We all know what *you* think, dearie," Lottie Dixon interrupted. "God knows you're always telling us. Maybe just this once you could spare us? Marianne's trying to say something."

Gen gulped coffee, spluttering, "Well! Who pushed your button, Miss Meeky-Mouse? Telling *me* off! Who do you think you are anyway?"

Maggie Neilsen intervened. "Just a minute, please. *I* know what Gen's just dying to say — that the new people probably unloaded a bunch of Rent-a-Suite junk like Mona Lisa did that time. Well, Gen, you must know by now that it was only temporary. And anyway, Mona Lisa couldn't care less who saw it."

Maggie had read her mind accurately, and annoyed, Gen shot back sullenly, "So what! Trash is trash, like certain people."

Marianne Fallon, anxious to keep to the agenda, yelled, "Oh stop this petty bickering, will you now? I'd like to get a word in edgewise, here. But first, Lottie, could we have some hot coffee? Mine's stone cold."

Lottie went to do her bidding. Marianne waited until all were served, then said, "Well, yesterday I just happened to be passing by Number 24 — walking Cookie, y'know — and the two of them were in the garage stacking empty cartons or something. I got a good look — I mean the door was wide open. *She* looked really dowdy to me. She had on a tacky old print blouse and torn dirty jeans. Her hair was a mess too, kind of scraggly, half tied up in a bandanna. *He's* good-looking though, handsome in a way, I guess. Grey hair — lots of grey hair — distinguished, know what I mean? I'd say they're both fifty plus.

Gen McMurdo laughed. "Why Marianne," she mocked, "sounds like you've got a crush on him. Oh my! 'Distinguished' and a lot of hair. Just your age too. Did you check the color of his eyes? And here I always thought you hated men."

"Oh shut up, Gen. All I'm trying to say is you have to wonder what a man like him sees in a mess like her."

That cinched the slim chance of Emily Grady being asked to join the Thursday Morning Koffee Klatch. Robert's good looks had no influence on this ladies-only group.

"Oh God, what a day!" Robert Grady collapsed on the sofa in his new living room. It was midnight and the moving men had just left. "Could anything else have possibly gone wrong?" He hand signed the words to give them expression, though Emily could lip read.

"Sure it could, dear Robert," she answered, "and it did. Look at me for instance. I'm a perfect mess and I don't think I'll ever recover from this move. I never worked so hard in all my life. The house was supposed to be clean and ready. Hah! So much for clean and ready. I don't call a ton of dust clean and ready."

"Emily, honey," Robert signed, "I'm so sorry I couldn't help more, damn it. That awful waiting and waiting was hard on you too."

"I know, Robert. Don't worry. That handyman will be here tomorrow. He'll finish everything up. But there is something we can do together, right now. It's not hard. Let's make the bed and fall into it."

Somewhere between point of departure and destination, the van carrying the Grady's belongings had stalled on 101. The movers pulled to the side of the freeway and put in a call for help. The trouble was minor, but knowing it would take a while for the company repair truck to come, the heavy lifters crawled in back to nap on furniture pads.

The repair made and the men refreshed by a two hour sleep, they revved up to hit the road again. The sun had set and a long haul loomed ahead, so it seemed fitting to stop at a roadside cafe for a meal and a few beers. This, too, took a while. And it took a while at the end of the journey to find Cardinal Court, which according to the map didn't exist.

By the time the last obstacle in the movers' progress was overcome, the ladies of the court were glued to summer reruns. Had they not been on the point of nodding off they would have been impressed by the quality of the Grady's material possessions. And Emily Grady would have been ardently recruited for coffee and Danish on Thursday mornings.

Robert and Emily, like Mona Lisa before them, couldn't have cared less what the ladies of the court thought about anything. Robert, recovering from surgery that left him with only one lung, needed all the vitality he could muster simply to breathe. He coped well enough during the days, but nights could be terrifying.

The Gradys had come to Cardinal Court to be near a medical complex that treated post-operative lung cancer patients. He hoped to learn breathing techniques to relieve the nighttime panics that left him gasping for air.

Emily, profoundly deaf from birth, was a light sleeper, but often failed to sense Robert's gasping struggle. A mechanical device was installed to wake her, but all too often it didn't.

They lived quietly at Number 24, Robert concentrating on learning the technique of breathing without panic during an attack. They made weekly therapy trips to the medical center.

They tried to lead as normal a life as possible. Emily swam in the pool and Robert puttered a little in the backyard, making flowers bloom with the help of a gardener. There were good times when they went out to dinner or a movie, when their grown children visited, and other relatives and friends dropped in. The Gradys dared to believe there was reason to hope.

But as summer sunshine gave away to fall rains, Robert began a gradual decline that started with nothing more than a casual notation on his medical folder at the clinic. Though he appeared to be doing well, he was in fact at the verge of a relapse. In time the gasping episodes and subsequent panicking occurred again, each seizure harder to endure. He refused to go into the hospital as his doctor suggested, telling Emily that once was enough, that hospitals were only places to die in.

Robert slid into a depression that Emily was afraid was despair. He brooded, hardly eating enough to sustain life, neglecting the garden he'd been proud of, spending the days in the room they used as a library, the door closed to Emily. He wrote copiously on a yellow legal pad he kept under lock and key, and held private conversations on the telephone.

Spring followed a wet and gloomy winter and one day Robert asked Emily to do some errands. Surprised, Emily saw the request as a good omen, a renewed interest in mundane things. A list of items to pick up at a hardware store, a number of books to take out at the library. "And stop at the bakery," he added as she was leaving. "Get a couple of those apple tarts we like. And don't hurry back, sweetheart. I'm fine today, really, so take your time."

Tentatively optimistic, Emily went off with the list. This has got to be a good sign, she thought. The hardware must mean he intends to fix something. He always liked fixing things. He wants to do some reading too. Fine. Wonderful. And of all things, apple tarts? When he's been eating practically nothing?

She lingered in the library deliberately. Perhaps he had sent her out to be alone for a change. Perhaps he was telling her she hovered over him too much.

Emily returned to find the narrow street clogged with official vehicles: a fire engine, three police cars, an ambulance. She knew at once that Robert's body was in the ambulance. She didn't need to be told that her husband had killed himself. Why he had sent her off on errands was now perfectly clear. And it wasn't to buy apple tarts.

With the Army 45 he had "liberated" on his discharge years before, Robert had blown off the top of his head in the backyard, in the garden he'd once been proud of. The blast had triggered three calls to 911.

He left no note, only the yellow legal pad placed conspicuously on the kitchen table. On it was scrawled, "Call Jerry." Jerry was his accountant, the other side of those private telephone conversations. The yellow legal pad instructed Emily on how to live without him. She didn't care that there was no farewell note for her. This terrible thing was beyond Robert's ability to put into words. Something he had to do, and she would know the Why of it.

Marianne Fallon, speaking for the ladies of the court, said, "We are *all* simply *aghast* at this *awful* news." Aghast but thrilled, she could have said, because this was the second exciting suicide the ladies had "been through" right at their front door, so to speak.

On reading a newspaper article on the death of Robert Grady, the ladies were chagrined to discover that both he and Emily were well-off and well-known. Scholarships were endowed in their names, funds were donated by them for the encouragement of young artists and musicians, and the poor and needy were not forgotten. Robert would be mourned, the article said, by hundreds of struggling students and artists, by all those the Gradys' generosity had helped along the way.

In their way, the ladies of the court mourned too, deeply regretting that they had not invited Emily to join the Thursday Morning Koffee Klatch.

"If only," Marianne Fallon lamented, "She had not looked so *dowdy* the day I saw her in the garage."

Enough Rope

K ate Kardis wanted to go far away from Cardinal Court, far from where her dear friend Jessie Donley's heart had stopped beating on the day of "The Company Picnic." That was Jessie's ironic way of referring to the Homeowner's Annual Labor Day Celebration.

Kate walked the familiar streets, the bassets Blossom and Twinkie tugging the leash to urge her on or making quick stops to sniff a bush or leave a message on a tree.

Jessie had been the focus of Kate's days. Now she had nowhere to go, nothing worthwhile to do. She didn't feel indispensable any more, except to her dogs. Jessie had needed her. Jessie had depended on her.

For Kate there would be no more afternoons at Number 24, the door firmly closed. Like a drawbridge shut tight against invaders who took too lively an interest in Jessie's former fame.

Kate and Jessie were deaf to the ringing bell and the knocking fists. It was their great pleasure to talk and laugh the afternoons away all by themselves alone, recalling memorable events of younger days. Jessie said some things were funny now that were anything *but* when they happened. She said being able to laugh now was a kind of dividend earned by growing older. "We've wept enough in our lives, Katie dear, it's time to laugh," Jessie said.

Kate sat at her kitchen table, Blossom and Twinkie sat at her feet, watching her face with sad eyes, making little sympathetic noises.

"All I have to do these days," she told them, "is cook meals I don't want to eat and wash up the dishes ... I get up and I go to bed ... that's about it ... no Jessie to do things for ... I loved that ... she loved to have me wait on her too ... stretched out in that tacky lounger ... 'Oh Kate, you really shouldn't, dearie,' she'd say with that little sideways grin of hers, and I'd say, 'My pleasure, Madam Queen.'"

The dogs listened, sympathetic to the sorrow in her voice. "I always had to tie you guys to her mailbox ... remember? ... poor Jessie had this dog-phobia thing ... afraid of dogs in general, not just you, understand? ... I know you never blamed her ... she couldn't help it, could she? Some people are just born that way, I guess."

Kate sobbed. "Oh Lord, nobody cares if I live or die!" The dogs whined softly and she patted their heads. "Present company excepted, of course."

Blossom and Twinkie wagged their bits of tails furiously, as if to say, Oh, if only we weren't so old and fat we'd jump right in your lap and comfort you! Don't you know we would if we could?

Kate moped through days and weeks of depression. Then a morning came at Number 13 when she awoke refreshed and euphoric; an unaccountable mood swing she didn't question. In a surge of energy she made a decision: the time had come to start living the rest of her life! All day long she pondered over different lifestyles that might be suitable and, toward evening, hit on one she saw as the solution to her dilemma. She laughed and clapped her hands like a child.

She would "sell" the house and fly off to Hawaii. She would be a "tutu," darkly tanned, lazing on the beach. (Once, on an island vacation, a little brown girl had solemnly told her, "A tutu is a grandma who wears a bikini.")

It's perfect! Kate told herself. A whole new life in a whole new place. Me, a tutu! Of course! It's exactly right! ... And to the delight of Blossom and Twinkie she danced around the kitchen, humming an Hawaiian melody, undulating her hips and hands in a somewhat arthritic hula-hula.

Kate Kardis knew her name was not on the deed to the house she lived in, a detail she didn't mention to the realtor she engaged to sell it. She told the dogs, "Somebody could buy it before they get wind of it," meaning the true owners, her late husband's stepchildren. Anything was possible, her mood swing was stuck at its manic phase. "Those kids are loaded," she said, "and we need money to get started in Hawaii. Just a down payment, maybe, before they find out. Just something to tide us over, y'know? But no matter what, I've still got some of my first husband's insurance money."

The dogs signaled approval of the plan by trying to lick her face, but settling for a couple of swipes at her knees.

Kate's Cardinal Court home was one of Duke's grand gestures. Her unlamented husband had liked to do things in a big way, as evidenced by the flowing champagne on their hasty honeymoon tour of Europe. For nine fuzzy, unsober days they sat in a bus with hardly a clue as to what country they were in at the moment. On the tenth day it was over and, hungover and exhausted, they knew at last exactly where they were. Back home and broke in the good old USA.

Since Duke had claimed to be broke after the European honeymoon, Kate was astonished when he presented her with the keys to a new home.

"Wait till you see it, Kate! It's in Cardinal Court. You'll love it. And it's paid for, no mortgage, cash on the line!"

"Cash on the line? Where did *you* get cash on the line? Just yesterday you asked me for money to buy gas because your credit card's been canceled. And you've been after me to dip into the insurance money I got when Jim died to pay the rent on this dump!" Kate rolled disbelieving eyes to the ceiling.

They were sitting in the living room of a small rented apartment. Duke got up and paced, looking for the right words. When the right words didn't come to him, he tried a winning and candid smile.

"Hey, you've got to trust me, sweetheart. I can still get my hands on a few bucks. We don't need his insurance money. I made a little investment, see, and it paid off. Come on, let me show you the house."

The "little investment" was a brilliant scheme Duke had devised for getting at the trust fund left to his adult stepchildren by their mother. He had to resist the temptation to tell Kate of its sheer genius and thus perhaps rekindle the esteem he felt she no longer held for him as a provider. But something told him this was not the means to that end. The house would do it though. She'd be a pushover for the house.

As soon as she saw it, Kate chose to file and forget the lies Duke had told her. Maybe his "little investment" had actually paid off; anyway she was sick of worrying about money. Duke had predicted that she'd love the house and she did.

Duke and Kate had settled into Number 13 Cardinal Court, she happily and he without an apparent qualm or scruple. But only a month had passed when Duke, lifting a glass to toast "Happy days!" fell over dead on the kidney-shaped coffee table, marking the moment with a permanent stain of Jack Daniels Black Label.

He left no Will. There was no way to leave his stepchildren's fortune to his wife. Or if there was a way, he hadn't figured it out yet.

Re-widowed, Kate consoled herself with the thought that at least this time she had a home, paid for cash on the line, no mortgage.

But it was not to be. Following Duke's sudden demise, his stepchildren called their lawyers, always suspicious of anything concerning Duke, even his dying. An investigation of the trust fund soon disclosed his chicanery. Kate was dismayed to learn that her house didn't belong to her after all, but to the stepchildren whose money had paid for it. A further shock came with the information that their money had also paid for the European honeymoon and the champagne that had blurred the landscape of the countries they may have visited.

Holding a family conference, Duke's stepchildren decided to let Kate live in the house, basing their decision on the fact that she too was a victim of his con-man tactics. The money involved was not a problem, they told Kate; they could easily absorb the loss, and as long as she lived in it they promised not to sell it.

Kate was already tutu-ing on the gold sands of Waikiki by the time Duke's stepchildren were shocked to learn of her ingratitude. At a second family conference it was decided to sell the house, since obviously she had not only abandoned it but tried to sell it, knowing full well it was not hers.

With Blossom and Twinkie in three months' quarantine, Kate's mood was still at the top of its emotional swing. She would be needing more space when the dogs were liberated; her tiny apartment simply wouldn't do. So she went househunting. She finally chose an ocean-front semi-mansion with a spectacular view, telling the owners she would soon return to close the deal, which was only a matter of transferring the proceeds of the sale of her Cardinal Court home. This was part dream, part lie, but a miracle might happen. Anything was possible.

But while the owners of the property waited, Kate had forgotten them completely. Her high spirits had deserted her, as quickly as they had come over her that morning in Cardinal Court. Something terrible, some disaster, was going to happen; she was sure of it. She stayed away from the beach, sitting or lying on her bed, waiting for the sky to fall. I won't think about anything, she said to herself. Then maybe this feeling will go away.

But the feeling didn't go away. Kate sunk deeper into depression as the pendulum swung closer to its nadir. She thought constantly of Jessie, of their amiable and devoted relationship; and wept. She thought of Duke, and wept because he had tried to make her happy, in his born-swindler fashion, and she had spitefully buried his ashes in a pet cemetery. She wept because she was tired and no longer young, and because she couldn't recall the face of her first husband. Weeping had become a way of life for Kate, and no Jessie was there to say, "You've wept enough, Katie dear, it's time to laugh."

Hawaii was expensive and the remaining insurance money dwindled fast. To cheer herself up, Kate went on shopping sprees, buying a dozen bikinis and sundresses at a time.

But trying on her new beachwear, she saw herself in the mirror, clearly, not blinded by fantasy. The cruel mirror reflected back an emaciated figure, wrinkled leathery skin, a once yellow-gold perm gone frizzy, arms and legs like sticks. The blunt image told her why she was not making much of a hit as a tutu; why she was not making friends on the beach who might be inclined to help her if it came to that. Another reason to weep, another loss.

"Oh, look at me!" she cried to the mirrored self, "Is this what a grandma in a bikini is supposed to look like? Oh God! I'm grotesque!"

But one thought sustained her. Something had prompted her to buy a round trip plane ticket to Hawaii, now a lonely place, a mistake, a crazy dream. She'd be better off starving where at least somebody knew her.

Despondent and penniless Kate returned to the mainland. The ultimate fate of Blossom and Twinkie she didn't divulge, or how and where she was living, when occasionally she appeared in Cardinal Court, dropping in on those onetime neighbors who had jealously snubbed her when Jessie was alive. She hinted to them that if a spare bed happened to be available, perhaps she could occupy it?

No offers were forthcoming, but someone spoke of a friend needing a housesitter while on vacation. Kate applied and got the job.

During the housesitting stint she called on an old friend. Dolly and Kate were inseparable best friends as children. People said, "If you see Dolly you're bound to see Kate, and vice versa, of course."

Dolly, too, was now widowed, but quite well-off. Kate's unhappy predicament touched her and, still fond of her long ago best friend, she offered to take her into her Peninsula home. It didn't take much persuasion. Kate was desperate for a place to lay her head.

Dolly structured her time with different activities she hoped would interest Kate: square dancing, lectures, singing in the church choir and tai chi at the local Community College. She tried to involve her with people she knew, but nothing came of it.

Kate had lived in her house for a month or two when Dolly began to wonder if what she had diagnosed as simply a little melancholy that time would heal was actually mental illness. She urged Kate to see a doctor. "You mean a shrink?" Kate asked. "Don't worry, I'm not a nut case. It's just that I'm tired all the time. I'll be all right in a little while." So Dolly tried not to worry when Kate began to lie in bed all day.

One night when Dolly was out swinging her partner in a hoe-down, Kate found a length of clothesline in the basement. She stood on a discarded kitchen chair and threw the rope over an exposed beam. One end she fashioned into a kind of noose, not too professional but close enough for her purpose. The other end she slip-knotted and pulled tight against the beam. She dropped the noose over her head and around her neck and kicked over the chair.

When Dolly found her she was quite dead.

Marianne Fallon was first to read the death notice: Kardis, Kate, suddenly in San Mateo. The newspaper dropped from her hands and she grabbed the phone to call the woman who had hired Kate to housesit. She got a name and a phone number. The address didn't interest her.

Dolly was distraught when Marianne called, and assuming her to be a close friend from the old neighborhood she impulsively burst into a description of the rope, the overturned chair, and Kate's lifeless body hanging from a ceiling beam. Marianne took in the details avidly, with a great show of ersatz sympathy.

Dolly said, "If you and anyone else from Cardinal Court care to come, there'll be a memorial service at the funeral home." Perhaps Marianne knew, she added, that Kate had sometimes called a Spiritual Advisor, a 75¢ a minute resource for people in need of an uplifting recorded message. Dolly had contacted the Spiritual Advisor in person, and she had agreed to conduct the ceremony. On behalf of the ladies of the court, Marianne accepted the invitation.

Her hand shook as she dialed Gen McMurdo. "Listen! You're not going to believe it! Kate Kardis is dead! Killed herself! My God, she hung herself!"

"No! I don't believe it! Really? How do you know? Tell me!"

"Never mind that now. The thing is, we're all supposed to go to a memorial tomorrow, so we've got to call everybody right away. You want to go, don't you?"

"I wouldn't miss it! I'll call Joannie and Maggie. You call Lottie. Call Mona Lisa too. Go ahead, it won't kill you. She liked Kate."

The casket was open. Kate was dressed in the pink bridesmaid's outfit she wore at Mona Lisa's wedding. The Hawaiian sun had tanned her still face and folded hands. The mortician's artistry had smoothed out the wrinkled skin and skillfully tamed her frizzy hair. She looked young and guileless.

The Spiritual Advisor, a stern-faced woman, was at a loss. In a whisper that carried to the ladies of the court gathered around the coffin staring at Kate's throat, she told Dolly her prepared remarks wouldn't suit the case at all. She said it was her firm conviction that Hell's fire awaited those who dared to take their own lives, and she was very sorry Dolly hadn't mentioned this iniquitous detail until after she had arrived.

Dolly sobbed, and the Advisor, since she was there anyway and had pocketed a fee, rattled off something about God's justice and left it at that.

Only Dolly and the ladies had come to the service, no one else. Only Dolly and Mona Lisa had sent flowers and the "slumber" room was bleak and cold.

Gen McMurdo leaned to peer into the casket. She nudged Marianne Fallon. "Can you see the rope marks? I can't."

"Shush!" Marianne answered in a low voice. "I swear to God, Gen, you haven't got the manners of an oaf! Can't you ever act like a civilized person?"

"Oh yeah? And I suppose you weren't looking for rope marks? I suppose you came here because you were so crazy about her, not just because you're curious?"

Lottie Dixon said, "Well, I admit I looked, but really, I didn't dislike her like you-all. In fact, I kind of liked her. So there!"

Maggie Nielsen asked Joannie Dettner, "Do you think they put shoes on them? I mean, it seems like kind of a waste, doesn't it?"

"Oh my God, Maggie! The things you think of! How would I know?"

Dolly picked up enough of their sotto voce comments to decide that Kate's funeral was over. She moved protectively between the ladies and the casket. "I think you'd all better go now. I'm sure you won't want to go to the cemetery and it's time."

The ladies straggled to the door, uncertain whether or not they'd been dismissed. Mona Lisa had been standing quietly in the background. Now she waited for Dolly.

"Don't mind them," she said, "those harpies. Kate would have laughed at them. She was my bridesmaid, did you know that? I'm glad she kept the dress, she looked lovely in it."

"She did look nice, didn't she? I found it folded in tissue paper in a suitcase."

"Yes, she looked very, very nice. I missed Kate so much after Jessie Donley died and she stopped coming to my house. She didn't want to see anyone, I guess, even me. I tried calling and ringing her bell, but no answer. Then she went to Hawaii and that was that. It's too bad I was away when she came back. I knew something was wrong, but I didn't think ..."

"I know. I suspected something too, but she wouldn't let me help her. And now ... well ... she didn't even leave a note for me."

Mona Lisa took Dolly's arm and walked her to the door. "I'm going with you. To the cemetery."

"Oh, no thank you. It's cremation, actually. I only said that so those ghouls would go. But thanks for offering."

They said goodbye in the parking lot. It was time to leave Kate to the indifferent care of those who don't mind burning up useless corpses.

Afterword

Cardinal Court was written at the time, and in the place, where the stories are set. It is a "novel of manners" in the Jane Austen sense, with elements of existential fiction thrown in. It was written with an eye for irony — the "court ladies" and their machinations, for example.

Some of the social customs described here are hopelessly out of date — *koffee klatches* and stay-at-home wives, for example — but the people and events described are still vivid and recognizable.

The absence of children in the tales boils down to floor space. The Court's two-bedroom units were intended for older people with money who wanted to live by a golf course, often as a second home. As it turned out, few newcomers played or even cared about, golf, or had another home.

Gertrude Crocker witnessed it all in real time and condensed it into this slim volume of dark comic fiction.

It's 1962 at Cardinal Court. Moving vans come and go. And the dogs do bark.

Made in the USA
Las Vegas, NV
18 February 2021